LLOYD SALT

By EVAN THOMAS

"Everyone has a future, a tomorrow in which they strive to be better than the last. I'm here to make sure that future becomes a reality."

-Lloyd R. Salt

CHAP1TER

He was there, watching the materializing creature. He was called Ezekiel, his last name he never revealed. It was developing slowly now. Its vital organs were complete, and recently they had begun to receive brain signals. Success was at hand.

He looked at the tables surrounding him, the small tanks on them acting as graves for all their failures. At long last, they finally had a sentient beast. But suddenly the generation came to a halt. The building blocks of life ceased to build.

"What happened?!" he barked at the doctor beside him.

Victory was so close they couldn't afford another slip up now. Their creature had to be completed.

"Th- there's been a shortage," the doctor said, shrinking away from his captor. "Of cells. We have no more to work with."

"Go harvest more! We can't handle another failure."

"Even if there were any sources left it would take too long to find one. It would die before—"

"I know! Silence!"

The doctor did what he was told, having a wise fear of his master, who was now staring at the half-developed monster hooked up on the machine before them. And then the doctor saw it in his eyes. Plan B was official. "Insert human cells," he said, a sly grin playing at his lips. "Let's see how his genes react. There's nothing to lose now."

"Ok…" the doctor was getting hot. He had an idea where this was going. "It will no longer be an exact replica of course, but we should still be able to make it work. Who will we extract them from?"

"You know more about this creation than anyone else here. Why don't you get some from yourself, and insert them into the creature?" "Well," the doctor said, stalling a bit. "We could technically call it an animal. Just because it—"

"Is there a problem Alahn? If not, I would hustle and do as I ordered."

"Y- Yes sir. I will go retrieve a needle."

Alahn hurried off into another room. Ezekiel turned to a woman beside him.

"Veronica," He said. "Keep an eye on him. He is the only unwilling scientist we have gathered, and he will truly disagree on some things that are about to take place. We don't need him anymore and if he tries to escape, kill him. I prefer to keep him around as another experiment, but he cannot leave here alive."

Veronica nodded.

"What purpose will he serve as an experiment?" she asked.

"The needle I've set for him to retrieve," he began, his stony face focused on the developing body they were creating, "has been used on our creature to conduct some D.N.A. tests on it. I've had this in mind and never cleansed the needle. When he uses it on himself, he may get a little back wash…"

Veronica smiled.

"We're getting inhumane, aren't we?"

"Who isn't. Our goal will be achieved in any manner possible."

Alahn returned now, a bandage on his wrist and the needle full of cells in his hand. Carefully he conducted the inserting procedure and implanted the cells into the creature's body. Humanness now came into it, twisting its miserable existence further.

"That should do it," the doctor said, after disposing of the needle, and coming to his masters. "It should start generating once again."

"Perfect." He said. "Now you are free to go to your quarters doctor."

"Thank you, sir." Alahn headed for his tiny living compartment.

"We've located his son." Veronica said when he was out of sight. "In fact, he's hiding out in the cabin beside the lake."

"He's here?"

5

"According to my scouts, he seems to be searching for his father. However, everyone knows so little about the disappearance he's getting nowhere."

"Then leave him. He is of no bother to us yet."

A man walked in from the doors that led to the hall of the doctor's quarters.

"He's all locked in there for sure." The man said. "And don't worry we left it up to you to inform him."

"Good." He replied. He walked down the steps that led to the platform he was on and headed towards the doctor. "The perfect world is in reach."

***   ***

The family business was complicated. We weren't detectives, we weren't secret agents. We were people who wanted to fix the world, schooled in a secret location by an Agency of Central Intelligence. It was highly hidden, and highly secretive. We were widely known, but not for what we truly were. Now thirteen, I had been schooled by this organization since I was three.   This education which was much different from the public and the private school system had two graduations and I had come up on the first. Our finals differ from all others of course, like so many other things. The first was spending time in a foreign town, accompanied by an adult who had already succeeded in all the tests, and fix what was wrong with it. They called this a "term of stay". I stood in the waiting terminal watching for the train that would begin the whole trouble in Coated Coast. My one bag was clutched tightly in my hand as I listened to the talking of my parents who stood behind me. One called Andre the other called Atria.

"We're so proud of our boy," mother said, running her fingers through my hair. Like a lot of mothers, she was making a big deal about my leaving. "Remember you'll only be gone for a term. You'll see us again soon enough."

I did not bother to tell mom that it was her who needed consolation.

"Relax dear," father said, patting her on the back. "He'll be fine. I still remember my graduation test that took place in New York. It was fun to think I was unsupervised by my parents."

Mother frowned.

"At least he'll have some supervision," she said, "an adult who has already passed the tests."

Father rolled his eyes. Both he and I knew how little the guardian was actually with you, and the organization only sent them so the child could get access to things that required a "grown up" if needed. Mother knew just as well as we did, for she graduated once too, but we let her just try to convince herself not to worry. Back in the day she was a respected agent who had acrobatic skills that could take down even those with the highest of combat training. She was always sent on field missions that required taking down some group of people or another. This is how she got the nick name, "Agile Atria".

All those years of awesomeness have kept her lean and mean through motherhood, although it had turned her into a worrier. Dad on the other hand had gained much weight since his earlier days as his job was being the guy in the chair who would always be helping agents like my mom by hacking into systems, giving them the map layout of the place, telling them where to go and what to watch out for, stuff like that. All those years of sitting had made my dad not fat, but much more plump. I, on the other hand, did not know who I was going to be in our organization. I did know I had always liked the engineering side of things. I was a whiz when it came to fixing, creating, programming. I had no idea where that would lead, or if it was just an unimportant talent. My father hooked his arm around my mother's shoulders.

"He has been trained by our organization for a decade." Father said. "He knows how to handle himself."

"Just try to be safe." Mother replied.

My father noted how we certainly didn't join this business because it was safe. Sometimes mother's worrying got annoying, but she was just trying to protect me. There are worse things mothers can do. I heard someone behind me saying "excuse me" and turned to find a tall man wearing a dapper cap pushing in between my parents. He didn't even bother trying to dodge me and his left arm slammed into mine as he was walking at a rather fast pace. He continued off towards the train that had just pulled in, without as much as a word of recognition. My mother started saying something, but I was more interested in the small object that had fluttered out of the man's pocket onto the ground.

"Hold on," I said to her.

Had I known it would be the last words they heard from me until after my long term, I would have chosen them more wisely. I picked up the green hundred-dollar bill that the man had dropped and hurried off after him. No one deserves to lose that amount of money no matter how rude. The train door opened, and the man was about to step in. It was just me and him. Apparently wherever this train headed wasn't too popular. I continued to alert the man about what he had dropped—as he planned I would. Normally one would accept the cash with a grateful thanks. What happened this time was the man turned around and accepted the large sum of money and smiled that smile that meant everything, and nothing. And that's when I recognized him, he grabbed me by the elbows and wrenched me into the train with him just before the doors closed.

It was a hard shove, and I stumbled a bit inside the train. The man was standing there with no certain expression on his face, as I often saw him with. I knew exactly who he was now. The thin mustache, blocky chin, sky blue eyes, the features were all there. He had been my enemy for a year now, ever since he gave me my first A- on my report card. He was the giver of homework, user of long words, and strictest person I ever met. Professor Quanton, my physics teacher.

He sat down in one of the small wooden chairs the train provided while keeping his eyes trained on me. I did not sit down.

In fact, I held his gaze looking as seriously as possible.

"Professor Quanton." I said.

"Lloyd Salt."

The train sounded its whistle and started off. Now I sat down in the isle across from my teacher. Out the window I saw the two figures of my parents pass by, then the brick wall of the tunnel leading to the outside track. I would not see them until after my term, almost not at all. The tunnel ended and the train entered a sunny day in the city of Chicago.

"I could've kept the money."

"But you were trained to do otherwise."

"My belongings are still back at the station."

"You don't need them."

"You cut me off from my parents. Why?"

While it was known that our organization will do unexpected things as part of your training, so you can learn to adapt to situations as you go, I was not impressed with the event they just pulled on me. I was supposed to know where I would be relocated before I boarded the train, but I was never informed. I didn't have any of my belongings with me, and only twenty dollars in my left pocket. And my conversation with my parents was cut off as if not allowed.

Quanton rested his chin on his fist and looked out the window.

"Parents never understand what we're doing here," he began. "Even those trained by us as well. You don't need any of their input going into your mission."

"Will I be able to communicate with them?"

"Not unless we are monitoring it."

"Couldn't even let me say goodbye, huh?"

The train must have run over something bumpy, as the tables that rested over our seats, vibrated and made a rattling noise. Quanton looked back at me.

"The mission is to be unsupervised." He said. "The less time you have around adults, the better. Especially family who can easily persuade you." This is how conversations with people I thought were convinced that they were smarter than me went. My asking relentless questions and pointing out any flaws in their decisions to down grade them. Many have found that I have a stunning lack of respect for authority. I did not always think I'm to be more clever than they, but I sure wanted them to know they weren't talking to any slack. I decided to drop the parent's conversation. My organization would do things for their own reasons even if it made no sense to me. Besides, I could talk to my parents all I wished after the term. Instead

I asked something that had been on my mind since before the train station.

"Where am I being located?"

Quanton seemed to either think, or just take his time in responding. But before he did, a matron came in holding a silver platter with teacups sitting upon it.

"Complementary tea?" she asked.

I shrugged and said, "Why not?"

She placed a teacup on the mini table in front of me and did the same for Quanton. When she left we resumed our conversation.

"Here," Quanton said, tossing me a yellow folder from the suitcase that sat at his feet with some papers and newspaper articles inside. "This will give you any necessary knowledge you should need."

"And you couldn't tell me this before, why?" I asked opening the folder. Clouds of steam rose from my teacup and into my face. I had never smelled a tea like it before.

Quanton seemed to have to consider his answer.

"To tell the truth," my professor said. "We weren't sure your parents would be on board with where you would be going. It's quite far upstate and many have never visited it."

"Coated Coast? I've never heard of that place before."

"Many haven't."

"These newspaper articles are like from fifty years ago. What's the deal with that?"

The steam had thinned a little but was still relentlessly pouring out of my cup. From the scenery outside of my window I knew we were not near the part of Chicago where I lived and were probably on the verge of crossing over into another town. When Quanton spoke again I couldn't tell if he was more tired of my grilling him with questions or answering them. "This town wasn't super populated in the first place," he said. "But there was a fall in its economy some years back that left it the most underlived place in the state, maybe the country. The place doesn't distribute newspapers anymore and hardly produces what got it started in the first place, sugar producing water."

I arched my eyebrows at him. His last sentence sounded like oxymoron. "It's a phenomenon that has scientists baffled. The town is so insignificant now that, like you, not many have heard of its legendary water-sugar."

I spread out the folder Quanton had given me onto the table pushing my strange smelling tea to the side. I found a map of Coated Coast that portrayed the small town in color. In the dead center there was a large circular body of water and the town was built around it.

"Amazing as it is," my professor continued. "Tests have proven the lake inside the town is just ordinary fresh water, and yet it generates the purest of sugar. This is how the town was built, the Sugar Industry starting it all basically. It supplied people with jobs and the town grew larger. Soon other shops and business centers sprung up along with aquariums displaying the fish found in the sugar emitting lake. People visited just to have a taste of its delicious sugar. It got the name Coated Coast from the term, Sugar Coated." As he was explaining I was looking through the contents of the folder. It mostly had papers with pictures of different parts of the town and what the newspapers said lined up with what my professor was saying.

"So, what happened?" I inquired. "What major economical fail did it have that the town just…. faded away?"

"The sugar." Quanton replied. "It was drained out from the big lake and didn't replenish. At least not in near enough quantities. There's still a little sugar but not enough to make any profit. The Sugar Industry shut down and so did the town with it. Shops gone, homes forgotten for years until hardly anyone remembers it now. The residents there have been there all their lives, as nobody new ever moves in. Of course, it wasn't just the fail of the Sugar Industry…"

I suspected another long explanation, so I picked up my teacup and sat back in my chair. Before I took a sip of my tea, I smelt a big whiff of it trying to identify what I may be smelling. It had always smelt different than other teas since the matron gave it to me. The smell was not natural I decided and did not drink it just yet. Who would attempt to poison me on this train? I had a pretty good idea of who. Opening the window beside me, I dumped the tea out into the grass we were currently passing. It was a good day out there, warm and sunny. I knew that would not last long as winter was coming soon. When the window was shut and I turned back to facing Quanton, I noticed he had stopped talking.

"Clever." I said. "What was that? The preliminary test?"

Quanton didn't even pretend he hadn't set up the tea having Chloroform in it.

"In a sense." He answered. "If one is not smart enough to avoid poisoning, he or she will immediately fail the test. If you had drunken that tea Salt, you would have been sent home, and most likely never get a good position in our organization. By not sipping that tea you just changed your life."

That was Prof. Quanton. Always talking about chain reactions. However, if I knew what was in store for me at Coated Coast, I may have rather drunk the tea. I still marveled at how Quanton's emotions never seemed to change or show. Ever since we had been on this train his face and words had been in a single monotone. I guess I wasn't allowing him to see my feelings either. Quanton was now relaxingly sipping his tea, apparently not worrying about it having been drugged. When he was finished, he continued with his story as though nothing happened in between.

"Although the town took a major blow from the sugar shortage, just the absence of sugar was not alone the cause of its downfall." The physics teacher carried on. "You see, the family that was the head of the Sugar Industry knew that their downfall was imminent with the absence of the water-sugar. So they decided to cheat the people. They invested in *normal* sugar, but put in containers of their own, and marketed it to people saying they should invest in it so together they could get the town running again. The town jumped on it and the citizens poured their resources into the scam. The Sugar Industry family got their money back and moved out of town before the people realized what happened. When they figured it out though, boy were they angry. They ran from town, they cursed the Sugar Industry's name, and the worst off even committed suicide. Since then Coated Coast has been nothing but a scrap of inhabitants unable to get away."

I had learned enough about Coated Coast. Closing the folder, I handed it back to Quanton who returned it to his suitcase.

"You certainly did your homework." I commented.

Knowing things is the key to this profession." He replied, with that expression about him. Anyone who's ever had a teacher knows what I'm talking about.

The train screeched to halt, and the whistle sounded.

"That's my stop." Quanton said, standing with suitcase in hand. "Have your wits about you, and remember, your term is under surveillance." With that he stood and went into the car in front of us and disappeared from view. Soon the train whistle sounded again, and I was back on my way. Not long after the matron returned and collected our empty cups and saucers.

She did not smile or say "hi" and neither did I.

***   ***

When my physics teacher said I was being located upstate, he meant it. Though the train ride wasn't gruelingly long, when I emerged from the tiny compartment, I could tell I wasn't anywhere near home. Trains travel fast and I had ridden for about an hour. It was surprising that the station I emerged in looked even older and more rickety than the small train I had ridden on. The dim light bulbs on the ceiling looked like they had flies stuck in them for a century and the chips and stains on the dirty tiles below my feet could have been in that condition since a date far before now. I glanced around the room I was presently standing in, looking for anyone who might be a guardian for a kid on a test for a secret organization. I was alone except for a receptionist at a wooden desk at the far wall next to the doors that led outside. I heard the train moving on as I walked up to the small desk with a heavyset woman trying to unsuccessfully sweep dirt away from her feet with a broom from 1950.

"Excuse me?" I said, prying her attention away from the floor and onto me.

"Has anyone been waiting for someone today?"

"You're the first to step in here today lad." She said, her gruff, scraggly voice making it clear she had smoked in her life.

I heard the doors to the right of us open, and a tall slender woman with flowy blonde hair walked in. She wore tight black pants with a looser but still skintight black sweatshirt.

"Rook," she said. "You ready?"

Of course, she knew my middle name.

"Waiting on you." I replied and stepped through the double doors into a town I did not know, with a woman I had not met, into a mystery where no one could win.

***   ***

Alahn toyed with the idea of escaping. Of course, that was suicide but was there anything to lose now? His humanness was already slipping away, so in theory he should just go for it and try for the best.

No. I've got to hang in here for my son.

The once respected doctor stretched out on his cheap cot, the only tool for sleeping provided. He remembered the days when he used his gifted genius to save lives, instead of creating them for some mad man. The creature was out of his hands now and would soon be used for whatever nefarious purpose that man Ezekiel had for it. Alahn sat up and let his feet touch the floor. The rest of his cell was empty, save for a little table and chair where food was occasionally set for him. He began to feel a throb in his left arm.

No... not again.

Ever since he had transferred some of his cells into the beast they were creating and found out that the needle contained samples of its cells as well, he had been undergoing something he could only describe as mutations. At first it had been nearly too much to bear, with every passing day bits of his humanity slipping away. This man, Ezekiel, had already stripped him of everything else, his family, his occupation, his nobility, and for all the world knew his existence. Now, however, Alahn had come to terms with his fate and simply bore the pain of this transformation with as much confidence as he could muster. His mutations were becoming more frequent, and they all started like this. The heartbeat in his arm got faster, then his veins began to bulge and discolor into a dark purple. Little scale like patches etched themselves along his wrist, adding to the ones that had been left behind from previous mutations. Alahn's arm surged with indescribable pain, each of his veins feeling as though they had been set ablaze. His veins continued to swell and began to protrude from his wrist, obtruding above, then returning back under the skin. The agony was so immense Alahn was hardly aware of his screaming. He stumbled around the room, his right shoulder banging into the hard wall. He fell to his knees and with his hand that was a blackish purple now, he clenched the metal chair in front of him just to keep control. He was aware of a crunching sound. His bones cracking against the chair. Slowly the pain subsided. His veins reverted to normal but remained purple this time. More scales were along his arm than before as well. Letting go of the chair Alahn wiped his brow with his right hand, which was dripping with sweat. Shakily he rose and returned to his cot. Before his heavy eyes closed, he caught notice of the metal chair he had been gripping. It wasn't his fingers that had been breaking. The top of the chair was crushed.

CHAP2TER

Quanton was on the drive back homeward when he received a conference call from the director.

"Salt is delivered?" he asked from the other end.

"Yes," Quanton replied turning on his earpiece. "He is set on Coated Coast with Karina."

"And his parents?"

"They were separated before they broke down and warned him. All communications between them and the boy will either be directed by us or non-existent."

"Then it is all in line. And I suspect your people are in place?"

"Affirmative."

"Very well. On my comm—"

"Cyrus?"

"What?"

"How will this boy accomplish any more than we have?"

"Though our phones are most likely secure, I'd rather explain in person. Meet me at the complex."

"See you there, commander."

***   ***

The tiny green buggy my guardian owned sped down the empty streets. Like Quanton had said, it was indeed very lowly populated. Any houses that weren't crumbled foundations looked like they had been there since the nineteenth century. I could tell the road had an arc and if you drove long enough, we'd end up back where we were now. No doubt it circled around the lake I had seen in the newspaper article. I glanced at the woman sitting to the left of me driving our little car. From my brief conversations with her so far, I had gathered that she was a field agent like my mother and was used for the operations with punching and kicking. However, that did not mean she didn't value herself as a smart person. Her name was Karina.

"Derelict," Karina said. "That's what this town is Rook. But I wouldn't expect you to know what that means. *Derelict* means abandoned, deserted—"

I *did* know what derelict means. I also knew my name was Lloyd not Rook.

Calling me by my middle name must make her feel like she's in a power seat.

Karina was driving and putting on make-up, a habit I now found dangerous.

She was a decent looking person, though I would never admit that to her.

"What's the case?" I asked her, interrupting her story of how she "courageously" busted some crooks who were hiding in a *derelict* warehouse. "Aren't you supposed to tell me what's wrong here? What's the mystery? What's the problem? I'm sick of you guys keeping me in the dark and revealing information as we go on."

"Impatience." Karina said. "Not a good quality in interns Rook. Let us at least get unpacked at where we are staying first."

Where you will get unpacked. I don't have the luxury of carrying my own stuff.

I had begun to get a grudge towards my organization as none of this had gone how I had imagined, and I said so.

"The world isn't how we planned Rook." She said, finally satisfied with her face and packing her makeup products back in her purse. "But it's where you live, and it don't matter if you thought it that way or not."

I wonder if she was told to irritate me.

"I'd appreciate it if you'd call me *Lloyd* and not *Rook.*" I said, not knowing what else to say. "I'd appreciate it if you gave me some more respect," Karina shot back, "and stay quiet for the rest of the ride."

That wasn't hard. There wasn't much of a ride left. We passed by some more shabby houses, a couple of shady gas stations, and a rundown supermarket. I wondered what was wrong in this little town. Masked thug steals twenty dollars from supermarket cash

22

register? My association wouldn't bother to send anyone for that. If there was some big mystery, I couldn't imagine what it was. I guess the town itself was though. What's the deal with the water-sugar? Why is it called Coated Coast if there's only a big lake in the middle? We came up on something that looked like it used to be a nice hotel and parked in the large parking lot it offered.

"Get acquainted, Rook," Karina said, stepping out of the green buggy. "This is your home for the rest of your term."

I followed her inside the old hotel. It seemed like it had about four floors and once looked impressive. Now, the paint was all chipped and the roof shingles were falling off. We entered a small lobby with thin red carpet spanned out on the floor. There was a rectangular wooden table towards the left corner with a set of cushioned chairs and a wooden desk by the right corner with a desk clerk standing behind it. He had a thin gray beard and sported some casual jeans and a black striped sweater. Walking up to the desk, Karina asked him for adjoining rooms.

"Certainly," he said, grabbing a random set of keys from a bowl in front of him and handing them to Karina. "I think those keys are for the last room on floor four."

Karina nodded.

"And how much per night?" she asked.

The clerk gave a dismissive wave.

"No one got money here anymore," he said. "Just drop a couple hundred dollars when you head out."

Karina said thanks, then I followed her up four flights of stairs and down a hallway to get to our rooms. They were almost as bad as I imagined them to be. Separated by a door, our rooms were identical; a small bathroom, a twin bed, crummy floors, stained walls, but the sheets were actually quite nice. I had nothing to unload so while Karina was unpacking, I just looked out the window. We were on the top floor and had a good view of the area. Unfortunately the area wasn't much to look at. When Karina was all set, she called me into her room, and I hoped I would finally learn what I was doing here. I was disappointed.

"This is your term, Rook." She said. "You've been asking why you're here, but it's up to you to figure it out. I can no longer help you. You're here, it's your term, and it just started."

Great. Completely up to me, a thirteen-year-old, to save a town and survive.

At least I'm a thirteen-year-old who was trained for this.

"Well," Karina continued. "Don't dawdle. Get to it."

She opened the door and was about to start down the hallway to who knows where, but I stopped her.

"Why?" I asked. "Am I under some kind of time limit too?"

"I'd stop asking questions," she replied. "And start finding answers."

Then she shut the door and left me alone in the room. I waited awhile before leaving as I did not want to run into Karina wherever she was going. After ten minutes or so I decided to head out and try to make some progress. So my term had begun.

***   ***

I concluded that the best way to start looking for ways to pass my term would be to walk around town as a newcomer who people would tell things to. For how under populated and shabby Coated Coast was, it was actually quite big. It took me a good walk to get to the main part of town if you could call it that. It was still quiet and empty but at least people could be seen. "Excuse me," I asked a man who looked like he was in his mid-sixties, sitting on an old wooden bench with his dog. "But do you know the way to the old Sugar Industry building?"

He looked up at me, and so did his tiny dog. It looked like a silver poodle. "Kid," he said in a gruff voice. "Just walk. The way this town is curved over and around that lake you can get anywhere if you just walk far enough." I could see the man's philosophy, but the town wasn't a thin strand of buildings around some lake. It had thickness to it and while I may be able to get to any section of the town by walking forward, I did not want to spend all day scoping out every segment of the town.

"Right," I said. "But see, I want to get there quickly. If you have any specific instructions that would be—"

"Come on," he said standing up from his perch. His dog obediently jumped down and stood by his side. "I've haven't anything to do since my retirement anyhow. Follow me, I'll show ya."

"Thank you, sir." I replied, walking beside him. He was walking at a slow pace but no slower than I would expect from a man his age.

"Yeah, yeah," he said with a wave of his hand. "The name's Anderson by the way. Folks around here call me "old Andy".

"Lloyd." I said, accepting the hand shake his right hand was offering.

"Ah." He replied. "So, Lloyd, what business do you have at the old Sugar Industry?"

The truth wasn't to be told in this scenario.

"I'm new here," I said instead. "And I hear that used to be the spotlight in this town. Just wanted to check it out."

Anderson grunted.

"That building was the start of this town and the end of it." He said. "Nothing in there anymore 'cept that family living inside."

We stepped aside for a couple who was hurrying by and walked past a small bank.

"People are living there?" I asked. "But I thought the family who ran the company moved out of town."

Anderson looked at me inquisitively and I could have sworn his dog did too. "You know a lot 'bout this old place for never coming here before." He said, though he didn't sound the least bit suspicious. "But yes, they did. See that bank we just passed? The owner bought the property and lives there with his maid servants and grown up son. He's bed ridden now and that son of his runs the bank."

We must have been far away from that so called "Sugar Industry building" as we were still walking the curved sidewalk. A station wagon sped down the road beside us, the first car I'd seen all day.

"So, he's one of the richer people in town?" I assumed.

Anderson nodded.

"The richest. Had enough spendin' money to turn that factory into a cozy home."

"And he would know a lot about this town, right?"

"Far as I'm concerned, I know enough about this place I could give you a history lesson. But he is one of the town's longest staying residents nowadays."

He looked at me a moment as if studying me.

"Where's your parents' boy?" he was saying. "You look no more than fourteen, and you roaming the streets of a new place yourself?"

"I can handle myself." I replied. "My parents know that."

Anderson either had the same experience as a kid or let his kids do the same things, as he nodded and smiled with a knowing look. A building much larger than the rest came into view.

"There she is." Anderson said. "If you're planning on meeting the family don't expect to feel at home. It's just how they are."

"Thanks for the guide, Anderson." I said. "I would tip you, but my money isn't flowing these days..."

"Its fine, its fine." Anderson said, scooping up his tiny dog and turning around. "Nice meeting ya Lloyd. I'm in the shabby yellow house if you want to drop by."

I doubted I'd ever drop by, but I nodded. I walked up the tar driveway, and onto the welcome mat of the building that would later stage something important. I rang the doorbell and after hearing it echo around the house for a few seconds, a tall woman wearing a maid's uniform opened the door. "Hello." She said without a smile. "This is Mr. Richard's home. What business do you have here?"

"I'm here to see Mr. Richards." I replied, realizing I was just now learning his name. "I'm the boy he sent for."

That was a risk. The maid's expression lightened a bit.

"So, your Earl Alten!" she said. "Mr. Richards has requested your visit multiple times. Word has gotten to you eh?"

This wasn't how I planned to convince her.

"It's a small town." I said. "So, do you know what he needs me for?"

"I'd ask him yourself."

She opened the door fully, and I walked in. It was hard to believe this place was ever a factory. It looked like a classic rich man's home with fancy carpet and excessively long furniture.

"He's in his quarters, the first door when you go up the staircase." The maid continued, gesturing towards the stairway. "He doesn't really get out of bed these days, but he's still sharp minded and gets very irritated if you treat him like a failing old person."

28

"I'll keep that in mind." I said.

When I ascended the stairwell and headed a little way down the hall it led to, I found the door the maid had told me about. If the man had called for the boy named Earl Alten, he probably knew what he looked like better than that maid. So, I'll play my cards a bit differently this time. I knocked on the door as I walked in, not bothering to wait for acceptance. The room was quaint, windowless, with a hard-wooded floor, a small cushioned rocking chair in the corner, and a bed which Mr. Richards lay in. Beside the bed was a tray, with a mound of books on it, most likely how Mr. Richards spent his time.

"Shoot," I thought I heard him mumble as he quickly rolled down his sleeves. Perhaps in his old age he was embarrassed by the tattoos lining his arm that his shirt was now covering. "Nobody ever knocks anymore."

He looked up at me.

"Who are you?" he asked gruffly.

"The maid sent me in." I explained. "She seemed to think I was a fellow called Earl Alten."

"Earl Alten?" Mr. Richards said, sitting up a bit. "You sho' ain't him. No freckles, too long hair. So, who are you?"

"Rook." I decided. Maybe it would be good if not many people knew my real name. "I'm a newcomer around here, and I understand this place has a lot of history. I came here to maybe learn some things."

The maid had been right. He wasn't some crippled old man. Why was he bed ridden?

"Well," he said when he had swallowed. "This town isn't what it used to be thanks to this place back when it was a water-sugar producer, -

"Actually a nice man told me all about that." I said growing a little bit impatient. "What I was hoping to learn here was if you think this town would make a comeback, or if any opportunities might be available for an individual."

"That sounds like a mature concern for your age." Mr. Richards commented.

"But no, definitely not. There aren't any good opportunities for anyone here, and this place isn't going to get any better from what I know now. I would say this town will disappear entirely in the not so far future."

"Why would you say that?" I asked, hoping there was some obvious mystery I could solve and pass my term.

"You an interviewer boy? Maybe you are Earl after all, eh?"

"No sir, I'm not. I'm just honestly intrigued with this town."

"Well," he said, speaking quietly as if it were some secret. "If you ask me it has something to do with the disappearance, the robbery, and the murder.

Some say it's a passing crime wave, but I think they're all connected."

Now I was getting somewhere.

"Do you happen to know where these things took place?" "I still don't see why *you*'re concerned. They say the chump who disappeared is the father of Earl Alten who the maid mistook you for. He was doing a study on the lake when folks realized he had been gone for over a day. The robbery happened at a closed aquarium a little way from here, and the murder- I actually don't recall. That good enough for ya, boy?"

"So no opportunities," I recapped. "Bad future and a crime wave going on. Nice place. Well, I think I got what I need so if you don't mind I think I'll take my leave."

"Please." Mr. Richards said.

As I was exiting the room I heard him muttering something.

"Kids." He was saying under his breath. "They're all interested in grown up things."

When I was back in the main room of the house the maid was still there.

"Leaving all ready?" she asked.

"Yes." I said. "Thanks for your hospitality."

And with that I left the mansion before I could get asked any more probing questions. Back on the streets I tried to remember from which way I came.

***   ***

A small beep of a horn blasted away my thoughts. Turning towards the road I saw a small yellow taxicab. The window rolled down to reveal a young man's face.

"Hey," he said. "Need a ride?"

I was surprised this town even had a taxi agency, and I said so.

"Nah, it doesn't." the driver replied. "It's just me helping people out. My dad used to, but he went out of town to get a better job so I took it up." "Aren't you a little young to be driving?" I asked.

"Sixteen." He said. "Just got my license. So you want a lift or what?"

"I don't have any money."

"That's fine. The way income is in this town I let folks tell me a good story on the way, and I'll drive them for free."

I seated myself in the passenger's seat and told him to drive me to the hotel.

"Got it." The driver said. "I'm Danny by the way. You are?"

I had the feeling Danny was a good guy. I told him it was Lloyd.

"Nice to meet ya." Danny said, taking off. "So how 'bout that story?" I told him a tale of how a young lad was nearly drugged by his tea because a sleeping agent had been slipped in it while he was riding a train. He escaped with a woman called Katrina and was able to get home by the next day.

"Interesting." Was all Danny had to say.

After a few minutes more the car stopped, and Danny told me I had arrived at the hotel. After I told him thanks, I was out in the parking lot of our humble hotel. I thought of where I would go from here, with the knowledge I had obtained from Mr. Richards. But before I had time to get in or think further, a siren wailed out into the air. A police car drove up next me, and two policemen stepped out of it.

They were both plump, one had a bushy mustache, and the other had short curled hair. I could tell from their nametags that the man was named Doug, and the woman was named Marcene.

"Rook," Doug said. "You're gonna have to come with us."

***   ***

Quanton arrived back to Chicago in time to meet Cyrus at his office room.

"So," Quanton was saying. "You were going to fill me in?" Cyrus nodded.

"Normally this information would only be for the elite."

"But?"

"But I'm promoting you."

"You are sir?"

"Yes. Though you and Lloyd are always trying to outwit each other like *children*," he said this with emphasis. "You and the boy seem to have a mutual understanding of each other. Like you asked earlier we do not expect the boy to accomplish any more than we have *inside,* but he may be just what we need to unlock the gate that stands between us and the barrier we're currently facing"

"So he's not our hero, he's not our bait, he's just our key."

"In a sense. From the information we retrieved from that girl, their operation will start in Coated Coast. Once Lloyd has done his work, hopefully he's alright to extract; then we can handle it."

"What do you mean "if he's alright"?"

"We're hoping he isn't killed or scarred, as he'll be in pretty deep on this.

This is *not* the average term we do for graduates."

"And he is only thirteen."

"He's the best option we got, no matter the age. If he escapes okay physically, there's no promise on what this'll do to him mentally."

"How do his parents feel about this?" "You were the one who had to separate them."

Quanton nodded.

"I'd be worried about my kid."

"They don't know that much about this mission. Lying to our own is tough, but what must be done must be done."

"Just how serious is this?"

"If that old document is reliable, we've got more responsibility than ever before."

 "So now that I'm part of the "elite" what's my job?"

"Like I said, you and Lloyd have a mutual understanding of each other. You're going to be the one who's with him after we extract him."

"So what are we up against?"

 "Evil, Quanton. And it's not just Coated Coast that's in danger."

"And Lloyd can help stop this danger, how?"

Cyrus sat forward and stared Quanton in the eyes.

"Before I go into detail, I need you to understand that all I'm about to say is true."

CHAP**3**TER

"It's amazing."

Ezekiel watched as the creature they were creating opened its eyes for the first time. No one in the history of the world had accomplished this. No one alive had seen this.

"It is." Veronica said, standing by his side. "Look, it's moving."

The creature extended its fully developed arm and pressed its appendage against the glass. Soon its dark purple hand slid off and its eyes shut again, as if the movement was exhausting. This one was actually going to work. Only its left hand was incomplete.

Ezekiel smiled.

"After years of planning my vision will finally be a reality."

"And let it be so." Veronica whispered.

Ezekiel was alerted of a call through vibrations in his pocket. Taking out his cellphone he answered the video call from an associate of his. A middle-aged man appeared on the screen.

"Stane." Ezekiel said. "Is this important?"

"Not yet," the man called Stane replied. "But it could be. It should be brought to your attention."

"And that is?"

"There's this kid, his name is Lloyd. I met him in town today. He seems to be sticking his nose in stuff that shouldn't concern an average kid his age.
You may want to keep an eye on him."

"Thank you for the report Stane." Ezekiel said. "Keep your position, and if the boy does become a problem find a subtle way to deal with him."

"I may have already set a solution up sir."

Ezekiel smiled.

"That's why I pay you Stane." He said. "We don't need any more curious brats jeopardizing our location."

Stane nodded.

"Still burning from the Zahna incident eh?" he replied.

"That was... an annoyance," Ezekiel agreed. "That does not need to repeat itself. But it is of more importance that you remain hidden than anything else. And don't forget your real mission."

"Oh, I haven't sir." Stane said. "He's ours any day now."

***   ***

Like the rest of the town the police station was unimpressive. The entire place was about the size of a convenience store and there were only two other cops besides the two that had taken me in. Besides us, there were two desks, a couple cabinets, and an old coffee machine. You could tell that this town didn't give much action to the police, so when there was a problem, they get all excited. Either that or they were jumpy from the crime wave consisting of a robbery, a disappearance, and a murder all happening in close succession.

"What did I do again?" I asked as they took pictures of me.

I noticed the maid that had let me into Mr. Richards home standing next to a cop answering questions.

"This maid of Bard Richards says that he claims you have stolen a possession of his. Not only that he called you by Rook, whereas the maid said you told her you were Earl Alten." Doug explained.

"However, we cannot find the missing object on you, and we didn't believe you had time to hide it, so we're still looking into this one."

"Sir," I said. "I did not steal anything of Mr. Richards'. If something went missing after I left, then it is pure coincidence."

"How do you explain your telling different names to the maid and Mr. Richards himself?"

"Ok, look." I began. "I do admit to bit of trickery. A man I was talking to led me to believe they weren't going to let me in unless I was someone they knew. I planned to trick the maid into thinking Mr. Richards sent for someone, and that someone was me."

"But why did you want to get in so bad?" Doug's partner Marcene asked.

The questions just kept firing at me.

"Because I was new! I happened to know that Mr. Richards was a long-term resident of this town so I thought I could get some great info about the place!" I said getting exasperated. If there's one thing about me, it's I absolutely can't stand false accusation.

"Hmmm," said Marcene. "Something still seems off. An expensive family heirloom went missing directly after you left, and you went to some strange measures to get inside someone's house. Seems to me it adds up to you're a thief just with no evidence against you yet."

I guess they're right about one thing, I thought as Doug pointed out to Marcene that she couldn't add anything without numbers. *I did take some unusual measures. I over think everything is my problem. What was it professor Quanton would always tell me? Don't outsmart yourself. That was it.*

"Doug, it was just an expression."

"I'm just saying, math never lies and to really add up something you need to have—"

"Guys," I interrupted their little expression squabble. I would witness more of those, as Marcene loved using expressions and Doug loved arguing them. "Don't you have more important things to investigate? Like the crime wave?"

"What do you know about that?" Marcene inquired. "Thought you said you were new."

"Well, you know," I replied. "Been hearing people talk. The disappearance shortly followed by a robbery, and then later a murder."

"Murder?" Doug asked sounding confused. "There's never been a murder in this town since I've been on the force."

"We've been looking into the disappearance and the robbery," Marcene agreed. "But never a murder."

"You sure?" I asked, a little surprised. "He sounded pretty certain..."

"Enough about other crimes!" Marcene said suddenly. "We're here to find out what's up with you and you're probably just distracting us! A girl has already just recently—"

A phone on one of the desks rang out.

"The emergency hotline!" A cop on the other side of the room exclaimed.

"Quick answer it!"

Doug hurriedly picked up the phone.

"Coated Coast police, what's the emergency?" he said into it.

The person on the other end was loud enough for everyone to hear. Her voice was scared and sounded like she was crying. "Please send someone," she cried. "There's been a murder!"

The room went silent. All eyes were on me.

"Where are you miss?" Doug said, still glaring at me.

"Downtown in the blue house next to the supermarket!" she said, her voice cracking." Please, come quick..."

"We'll be there as soon as we can." Doug said. "Hold on."

He put the phone down and put his police cap back on.

"You guys make sure he stays here." He said pointing to the other two cops in the room. "Come on Marcene there's a murder we need to investigate." And with that the two left the building. The sounds of an engine starting and taking off soon followed.

The officer who had alerted Doug about the phone approached me. His nametag read Mac.

"Boy," Mac said. "How on earth did you know of a murder before it happened?"

"I think the real question," I said. "Is how did Mr. Richards know of a murder before it occurred?"

"What are you talking about?" Mac asked.

"That's how I learned of the crime wave. He included a murder with the other crimes."

"How do we know you're not lying? You already stole something from Mr. Richards. And if you knew a murder was going to happen, maybe your part of some gang, huh?"

I ran my fingers through my hair. This had not been a great first day of my term.

"As far as I can tell," I replied slowly. "There is no proof that I stole anything out of that house. You can accuse me, but you cannot speak it as truth, or condemn me to anything."

"It had to have been you." The Mr. Richards maid said, pointing an accusing finger at me. "Nobody else came in today besides you!"

"Thank you for your input, miss," said the other officer with a nametag that read George. "You can leave now. We'll handle it from here."

She "hmphed" and left the building.

"What do you think George," Mac said. "The boy's right, we have no evidence against him, but his identity trickery and murder knowledge is strange. As well as the object went missing soon after he left."

"But we could not find the missing object on him, and when we caught up to him, he was just exiting a taxi." George added. "How could he have time to hide it, if he truly did steal it."

"Exactly." I said.

"Hold on," George said quickly. "Unless him and the taxi driver are in cahoots and he left it with him!"

These officers clearly weren't the most professional, the way they jumped to conclusions. I listened to them throw out some more ideas of how I could be guilty.

"Guys," I said my irritation growing. "Can we just slow down? I did not steal anything, and Mr. Richards was the one who told me of the murder, and I explained why I pretended to be Earl Alten. From my perspective I'm in the clear."

I was surprised I actually talked to police officers like that. The two law enforcers seemed to think for a bit. Soon Mac sighed.

"Fine." He said. "You're right. We've got nothing that says you did anything, only our suspicions. We'll let you go now but be warned. I'll be keeping an eye on you, and any more incidents you're coming right back here but for longer. Understand?"

"Yes sir." I said nodding. "And if you need to know more info about the murder, I suggest go see Mr. Richards."

I certainly will.

And after stating that I happily left the building, quite shocked they never asked me where my parental guardian was. Confusing thoughts of Mr. Richards and the murder filled my head all the way back to the hotel.

***   ***

When I had finally found my way back to the hotel, day had turned to evening. Karina was waiting for me in her room, and as soon as she heard me enter mine, she barged in through the door that connected us.

"Rook," she said with an annoyed tone. "Where have you been for so long?" "Karina, I've had enough of people calling me Rook for one day. I'd really be thankful if you'd call me Lloyd."

It'd been a long day, and taking forever to find where our hotel was, didn't make it any better.

"Wow." She said. "You're serious this time. Sorry. I just heard or read somewhere that calling a person by their middle name made you appear authoritative."

"Right." I said. Would I meet anyone mature on this term? "Well if you'll excuse me, I think I'll go to bed early. I'm exhausted and have a lot to think about..."

"Oh no you don't!" Karina snapped, her turn to be irritated. "I've been waiting out of courtesy for you before I went and got dinner. I'm starving.

What is it, like seven-thirty? You're definitely coming with me." We climbed back into the ugly green buggy and drove to the nearest restaurant. I wasn't going to argue with Karina, as truthfully I was pretty hungry as well. We pulled into a restaurant called The Mouthful and were soon seated in a booth next to some dirt ridden windows. The restaurant was actually bigger than I expected, but the shabbiness that ran throughout the town remained. Besides Karina and I, there was only one other family there.

"So," Karina said while looking over the menu. "Was your first day a success?"

"Not sure if I'd call it that..." I replied. "but besides getting arrested—"

"You got arrested?!"

"- and someone dying today it wasn't bad."

"Someone died!"

People at the other table began to look at us.

"Karina could you stop repeating me really loudly?"

"Hold on," she said putting her menu down. "How'd you get arrested? That's not going to be good on your grade. What on earth did you do?"

"It was just a mistaken suspicion," I explained. "That got to the cops who are very good at jumping to conclusions. I didn't actually do anything."

"But someone died?"

"Yes. A murder. The first in this town for apparently a very long time."

"Did you check it out?"

"I'm sure it'll be in the newspaper tomorrow. I'll find out about it the easy way."

Our waiter got to our table. I recognized him as Danny, the taxi driver.

"Danny." I said. "You work here too?"

"It's my night job." He replied. "Gotta get money, you know? Anyway, nice to see you Lloyd."

We ordered and were soon eating. After serving our food, Danny sat down beside me.

"So," he said. "You guys new? I've never seen you before."

"Yes." Karina said. "We're just visiting for a while."

"Visitors." Danny said smiling. "That's something we don't get often."

"Looks like it." I agreed. "It's too bad this town shut down. I mean, your lake produces sugar like the ocean produces salt." "Used to." Danny corrected. "Not so much anymore."

We finished our food and were about leave.

45

"Hey Danny," I asked before we left. "Is Mr. Richards a strange kind of guy?" "He's anti-social," Danny replied. "If that's what you mean. But I wouldn't say he's any weirder than anybody else in this town. Why you ask?" "He just said something today that struck me as odd. But I don't want to gossip. See you around Danny."

Karina and I returned to the hotel, and I gratefully accepted sleep when I laid down to go to bed.

There was evening and there was morning. I thought as I was dozing off. *The first day of Lloyd Salt's term.*

***   ***

Morning came soon. I was up and dressed much before Karina and used the time to slip away without getting into conversation with her. *On the agenda today,* I thought recapping what I had planned to do the night before; *A: Visit the lake which is also the disappearance site. B: Take a look at the aquarium that was robbed. C: Confront Mr. Richards about the murder. Yep, I'm booked.*

On the way out of the hotel, I looked for any newspapers I might be able to use to learn about the killing yesterday. To my dismay there were none. "The newspaper company shutdown a little while ago." The desk clerk said when I asked about a newspaper. "There wasn't enough money coming in to keep it going."

"This town doesn't even have a newspaper?" I said in disbelief. "Man, I miss Chicago."

"Yeah, well," the clerk replied. "That's why not many folks come here."

I thanked him for his service and exited the building, a bit disappointed. Since the town was built around the lake in a circular curve, all I should have to do is walk forward far enough and I would get to where I wanted to be. So, I did. Walking across a couple streets and weaving around some buildings.

The town was quiet with very little life as always. I managed to come to an empty lot that was filled with grass. Beyond that was a lake, almost perfectly circular, the grass around it following shape. I walked up to the brink of the lake and gazed out on it. The water was crystal clear, the most beautiful I'd ever seen. It was a small one though, and one could probably swim to the other side without getting too tired. Some way to the side of me, was a wooden structure that appeared to be some kind of a fort on the grass beside the water. Deciding to check it out, I began to run along the side of the lake. In a couple minutes I was there. Now that I was up close, I realized it was more of a cabin than a fort. It was in good condition too, besides the wood looking a little old. But that was the norm in this town anyway. There was a sign near the top of the wooden cabin that was broken and cracked, but from the letters you could decipher, I figured it said: Fresh Water-Sugar! $5 a bag! Perhaps this used to be a shop where you could purchase the once mysterious water-sugar. I opened the door and stepped inside. My hunch seemed to be correct, as there were many shelves lining the walls, and a desk with a rusted cash register on it. But these didn't hold my attention for long, because on the floor was something much more recent. In the far corner was a sleeping bag, a backpack, a couple of notebooks strewn on the floor, and a newspaper to the side. The newspaper couldn't have been native to the town for reasons the hotel desk clerk had explained to me earlier. Someone had been living here, and recently. Turning to leave before they returned, and I would be forced into talking to them, the headline on the newspaper caught my eye. It read: MAN GOES MISSING AFTER RESEARCH ON LAKE! Now *this* would be helpful. Not wanting to steal from most likely a homeless person, I delayed my exit to read the article. My hunch about the paper had been correct. It was from Springfield, telling of how a biology doctor who lived there, went missing:

A Doctor in biology, thirty-seven-year-old Alahn Alten vanished while conducting research on the Coated Pond. Divers have searched for his body on the Pond's floor but have found nothing. Any equipment he was using mysteriously vanished as well. "Drowning," the chief of police stated.

"Seems highly unlikely. His family has assured me he knew quite well how to swim. This leaves two options; he either purposefully ran away, or this was the result of a kidnapping." Authorities will continue searching for the reason behind his sudden disappearance.

Great. I thought, setting the newspaper back where I found it. *Now I know his name and due to the date at the bottom, about when he disappeared as well. Man, that was a few weeks ago. I wonder if the search parties have given up yet?*

With the info I had now gathered, I quickly left the old shop before I could be spotted by whoever it sheltered. As I headed back towards town, I was unaware of a boy who was watching me from behind the cabin.

***   ***

Back at the hotel, I used their *one* outdated computer to research the name I had just learned. He was indeed a doctor in biology, who worked at an institute in Springfield. I also got a picture of his face, which could be useful lest I encounter him. He was blue eyed, with short brown hair, with a very short beard. After logging the picture to my memory, there wasn't any more useful information available about him. But while I was on the computer, I decided to research the name *Bard Richards* as well. I didn't get much I didn't already know. He was rich, he remodeled the factory, all stuff I had learned from Anderson. There were some random bits of information like; "he never missed a Cubs game", things like that, that I didn't care about. One fact unsettled me for a reason I was still putting my finger on. It said:

Bard was firm believer in treating your body like a valuable possession, and spurned anything that would harm it, such as

49

smoking or the getting of tattoos. He neither smoked nor got a tattoo in his life and scolded his son who did both.

Why didn't that seem right? I thought back to when I visited Mr. Richards yesterday afternoon. The desk clerk answered a call from his phone. A woman exited the hotel. And suddenly I remembered. Closing out and shutting down the computer, I headed to the stairs to speak with Karina about a few things. Mr. Richards was certainly not who he claimed to be.

***   ***

"You've given me power!" Alahn shouted up at Ezekiel. He slid down his sleeve to reveal a purple scaly hand, his fingernails grown into sharp black claws. "I ripped that metal chair off the ground it was bolted too with this hand! I could break out of this confinement and kill you where you stand!"

Ezekiel shook his head from outside the extremely tough glass between them. The frequent mutations had begun to derange the doctor, an expected side effect.

"Oh, I doubt that doctor." Ezekiel said. "You think I didn't know what I was giving you? Your "confinement" as you call it, will not yield to your newfound power."

Suddenly Alahn lunged towards the glass and slammed it with his claws. He then dragged them down creating an awful scraping sound and leaving behind wide claw gashes.

"Someday it will." Alahn growled. "And you'll be sorry as I'm having my revenge."

"Even if you could escape Mr. Alten, I'm not sure it would be your best interest. Because you see I hold all the cards, and the ace happens to be your son."

Alahn stopped.

"You have Earl?" he said, his voice beginning to sound frightened.

"We certainly know where he is." Ezekiel replied. "And he'll be walking into our hands shortly. Unless you want him to be punished for the sins of the fathers, I'd remain contently where you are."

More scales were etching themselves along Alahn's neck and back.

"Where are those big words now?" Ezekiel taunted. "Weren't you going to kill me, or was that just for show?" Ezekiel snickered.

"You see, I'm too prepared Alahn." He continued. "There's nothing that will attempt to stop me that I cannot apprehend."

Alahn glared up at him in hatred, as Ezekiel just stood there, and smiled.

CHAP**4**TER

"Much about time travel is still highly theoretical," Quanton
explained to his class, "But that does not mean impossible. There
are many different theories on how one would accomplish time
travel, but today I will share the conclusion I myself have come too."
He began to draw on a dry erase board to get a picture in his
students' minds as he explained.

"You see, I believe that time is like a linear highway, spanning out
with all the events that ever have been, or will be."

Quanton drew a line with many different dates beside it, including
the present one, and future dates.

"Now as I see it, the time we are currently living in is like a container
we're trapped in, heading one way down the linear highway." To
show this he drew a box around the current date.

"If this were true, all one would have to do to get to a different time, would be to somehow break out of the container and advance or back track along the linear highway to get to one's desired time." Quanton then drew a hole in the container, and arrows pointing in either direction of the highway.

"How one would accomplish such a feat gets even more theoretical. Obviously, you would have to make it so that the time container could no longer, well, *contain* you. Some have speculated that going fast enough could rupture a hole in your current time that you could escape from, others suggesting that there are "leaks" in the container creating wormholes someone could stumble upon, possibly sound ideas."

He drew a speed scale going off the charts, and little holes inside the box.

"I have concluded that if one were to amass enough power, they could burst a hole in the time container and enter the linear highway. Power such as that of a dying star, what we call a super nova. Does anyone know what conclusion can be drawn from *this*?"

"Dying stars sometimes create blackholes." A slender boy wearing a thin black coat in the front said. "You're saying black holes are the key to time travel."

"Indeed, I am Drew." Quanton replied. "No person or machine have reached the center of a black hole. I believe that's an entry point into the linear highway."

"So, the black holes throughout the universe," Drew added, "are all gateways to any time."

"Exactly."

"If man could somehow harness the power of a supernova, or a star that they could create conditions like one, they could possibly have more control over it—"

"Slow down Drew," Quanton cut him off. "I'm teaching the lesson here. What Drew started is correct. If we were to harness power like that, in theory we could create a hole into the highway with more safe conditions than a black hole. Thus, making time travel possible."

Quanton looked over the class, the sea of faces over their desks, each student taking notes in his or her notebook, some copying the picture he had drawn.

"So, any questions?"

A tall blonde girl wearing a purple shirt in the back rose her hand.

"Yes, Jessica?"

"I'm curious," she began. "What your theory on changing events is. Can you mess up the original lay out by traveling back into the past, or were you always there anyway, so you couldn't?"

"Good thought Miss Jessica." Quanton said. "That has been debated many times. My thoughts are this; there are millions upon millions of outcomes for every event. On the linear highway our time container is on, it has intersections just like a regular road, except

54

occurring for every event, and millions of different paths to choose from. The time container is on a one-way path until a time traveler would change the standard events, forcing it to take a turn in one of the millions of roads there are. On this subject, I believe we are living on one of these such paths, as I'm sure in the future there are time travelers who have traveled to a time occurring before our era."

"So, you think we're living in a parallel universe?"

"Not a parallel universe, Jessica, but a possible outcome of *our* universe. I'm glad you brought that up though. Different universes, and different dimensions have been a theory for a long time now. Following my thoughts on the time continuum, I think the parallel universes, or the different dimensions are different possible outcomes of the creation of the universe. If there are indeed millions of different paths for every event, there must be for the creation of the universe as well. Think about it, in a different timeline, a possible outcome of the existence of the entire universe, who knows what creatures, or things could exist?"

"Fascinating." Drew commented. "And upon entering the linear highway you could enter such worlds?"

"I assume so." Quanton replied.

"But if it was only a *possible* outcome of the universe, how could you visit them?" Jessica asked.

Quanton smiled. He loved the opportunity to explain all his concepts and ideas, and he loved it when his students asked questions he had to answer. Besides Lloyd, Jessica and Drew were his top students; Drew always catching on and adding to the lesson and Jessica always asking intelligent questions. If Lloyd were here rather than off on his term, Quanton would have got some challenging questions, and be debated on his theories. How he enjoyed teaching those three.

"A valid wondering." Quanton answered. "But a bit simpler to explain, if you can understand it. The linear highway consists of all things that have, could, or would be. Time being linear, all these things have happened, and are all happening at once, even though we ourselves have not experienced it."

"Complicated." Was Jessica's response.

"But it makes sense." Drew said. "Although time travel could be a dangerous thing. With that kind of power someone could do massive damage."

"Damage," Jessica mumbled. "That's right! I had another question. On T.V. and in books people are all worried about damaging the time continuum. But the way you explained it, it doesn't seem as though you can. What are your thoughts on that?"

"I believe," Quanton began. "That time is like an organism, and like all organisms you can hurt it, *abuse* it. Creating too many entry holes into the linear highway, or a massive one, I believe could distort the fabric of reality, meshing all events that have been, could be, or will be, in turn linearizing everything. Our human minds couldn't possibly fathom such an event, and life would cease to exist, and exist again, in a constant loop of unchecked time released upon *everything*."

Besides Drew, all the students faces had a look of wonderment upon them.

"Everything would fall apart." Drew said.

"And when everything falls apart," Quanton replied. "Is there anything left?"

He had been waiting to say that. A bell rang out through the classroom, jumping up all the students from their seats.

"And that's class, folks." Quanton said. "You're all dismissed, and if you wish to debate any of my theories with me, I'm free during study hall. Next time it would be more enjoyable to hear more voices in addition to Jessica's and Drew's."

The class filed out of the room. Before he left Drew approached Quanton.

"If what you taught us is true," he said. "Humanity could learn so much from studying the linear highway. And as it's your job to study and add to the knowledge of this organization, I suppose you're working on proving your theory?"

"I don't believe you have the clearance code for me to say," Quanton replied. "But you can *theorize* anything you would like."

Drew nodded, and exited the classroom. Yes, indeed Quanton was working on proving his theory as he did with all of them. He was quite far off from it though. He sat down in his "teacher chair" and thought about what Cyrus had told him the day before. Did he believe it? Did he believe it enough to act on the commands Cyrus may give him? Quanton looked at his drawing board. Some would say the same things about what he had just told the class. But that was different. That was *science*, quantum physics, not... not like what Cyrus had told him. He sighed. Cyrus was the commander of this branch of the Central Intelligence, and Quanton would just have to hope he was correct about the past.

***   ***

CENTURIES AGO...

His name was Oliver Cast. He stood before a throng of people, most jeering at him, yelling things of disgrace towards him, as he was finally receiving judgement for his crimes. Some were quiet and solemn though, seeming on the verge of tears. His family was clearly disappointed in him.

My family, *Oliver thought.* What a joke. They create the most powerful crossbreed and they don't even want to utilize it.

Some time ago a couple fell in love. This would be of no significance if it were two of a kind, but this couple was the first marriage between humans and the cosmics. Some disapproved of love between the two species, others thinking true love comes in any form. Regardless of who was right, a male cosmic and a female human were married, and soon bore a child. The child was Oliver Cast. The cosmics had strange, sorceric like abilities, and the humans had incredibly intelligent brains to create, and establish new things. Oliver had the purple skin, and the cosmic powers of a cosmic, and the looks and supreme intelligence of a human. He was the most powerful being to walk the earth, and he saw what opportunities his power could bring. He tried to take charge of the earth, bring order of the natural chaos it wrought. He very nearly succeeded, making even the most powerful of leaders kneel by force. But with everyone against him, everyone too blind to see the perfect world he was creating, including his own mother and father, he was eventually defeated and captured. Now he stood before the judgement circle, rows of people gathered around on benches to see him get what he deserved. The judge strode into the center and stood in front of Oliver. The enchanted handcuffs they had put on him rendered Oliver's powers useless and prevented him from inflicting physical violence as well. Naturally now that he was helpless, the judge threw some taunts at him.

"Is this what you had in mind," he asked looking around the crowd, then back at him. Cosmics did not have mouths, so they communicated by telepathy, broadcasting their message the desired distance. "When you attempted to make all the kingdoms gather under you?"

The crowd cheered. Oliver glared at the judge. Judges of cosmics were often ones with great magical power, capable of casting a curse worthy of the crimes the accused had committed.

"Because I tell you, the actions you have committed will forever change every nation of the earth. You have forever scarred the relationship between the humans and the cosmics."

The crowd stopped cheering to listen. One side was of cosmics, the other side of men, both wanting to know what would become of their current peace. The judge continued.

"You Oliver Cast have prevented any more marriages between our species ever again in the future, and our entire partnership,"

Oliver could see his mother weeping on one side, his father having a look of regret on his face.

"Through you we have seen the true mind of the humans. You knew them better than us, and that is why you made your forces up of men instead of cosmics. With the great intelligence that humans use to create, they also use to conquer. The decision we have been wavering on was decided by your actions. We cosmics are creatures of peace, while you men are creatures of war. We have been watching your history and the recent events Oliver has cast on us we have come to a conclusion. The Elders of the cosmic race have declared, that the cosmics are leaving Earth!" Everyone gasped. Oliver remained silent. "We are taking the cosmic properties that we cast on your waters out, making this planet uninhabitable for cosmics. All cosmics that remain

alive are ordered to come with us. The Elders are currently spreading this message worldwide."

The two sides of the circle looked at each other, in disbelief that their partnership was about to end after years of being together.

"And as for you mister Cast!" the judge bellowed magic power gathering in his hands. "I condemn you of murder, destruction, and the disruption of the partnership between humans and cosmics. I judge you with this curse I am about to bestow upon you!"

He raised his hands and released the magic energy upon Oliver Cast.

"I strip you of your cosmic powers, and from any offspring you have, until one is worthy to wield it! I also condemn you to forever be an outcast, not welcome on any corner of the earth! You will not come with us on our departure, but instead be sent to a place where you must learn to survive and be isolated."

The handcuffs binding Oliver broke, but his cosmic powers were gone anyway. He was but a helpless human now.

"Before I send you to the place we have decided upon, do you have any last words to say for yourself?"

Oliver looked over the crowd and spoke to them for the first time.

"I tell you," he said. "You have managed to win today, but you have not won tomorrow. You never will. I may be defeated but others will see what I saw. Others will surely follow in my footsteps. Whether you admit it or not, it's not just humans, but also the cosmics that crave a master. Another will attempt to bring order to your natural chaos,

and once again you will be too scared to allow a change. I just hope
he succeeds. And one day when you are all under him, I just hope you
think of me, OLIVER CAST!" No one seemed phased by his dramatic
announcement.

"And that was his last declaration before being cast away." The judge
said.

"Now be gone, Mr. Cast."

A purple mist was released from the judge's fingers and wrapped
around Oliver concealing him completely. When it faded away, he was
gone, sent to whatever place on earth the judge had in mind. The
crowd would have cheered like they previously had been, but the news
of the cosmics leaving earth was still too fresh in their minds.

"On the subject of the cosmics' departure," the judge continued. "We
will leave in three days. We will cast a blind spot spell on all of
humanity, so that they remember nothing of our existence."

Oliver's mother was now crying. Her husband on the other side settling
for a look of pain.

"My last advice to you humans' is don't waste time on goodbyes you
won't remember."

And with that he left the stage. The people and cosmics soon filed out.
Oliver's mother ran and embraced her husband.

"I can't believe," she sobbed. "I'll never remember the love of my life."

"But I'll always remember you." The father of Oliver Cast said. "No
matter how far from home we go, I'll never forget you."

"And where is your home besides Earth?"

"Up there." He replied pointing to the sky. "Our true home is the cosmos."

***   ***

Three days later...

The Elders of the cosmics watched Earth fade in the distance as they rocketed through space. Using their mysterious cosmic powers, they flew themselves at speeds considered unachievable, leaving tales like comets behind them. The three were in close proximity to each other so they could discuss the current events as they always did.

"Though we leave we must not forget our true mission." The chairman of the group said. "To spread our existence across the entire universe. I suspect you two accomplished what we decided on?"

"Yes." The one to the left of him replied. "I made the little pond in the west capable of housing life for cosmics and placed a male and female cocoon inside. They will hatch in a few centuries and when fully grown the knowledge of what has passed will enter their minds. If they find the humans worthy by then, they will send a signal."

"As have I." the one to the right of him said. "I made capable of housing cosmic life the lost city submerged in the Atlantic sea. I too placed a male and female cocoon ready to hatch in a few centuries. They as well will unlock the knowledge that has passed when fully grown and will send us a signal if they find human life worthy in that time."

"Good." The chairman said. He looked back at Earth as it went out of view completely. *"Farewell Earth. If you are not found worthy when the centuries are up, we shall never return."*

***   ***

There was no cafeteria. That was much too loud and disorderly. Instead students were instructed to each bring their own lunches and eat in a designated area at various times. It was more efficient and less costly as far as Cyrus was concerned. The leader of the school for raising geniuses and critical thinkers on a mission to create a successful future, he made visits to the different schools under his leadership. Today was one such day, at the school with the intelligent physics teacher, Professor Quanton. They sat outside on a wooden table positioned so they could see through the lunchroom's window as they talked.

"This school has been my most successful." He said, hands folded atop the table. "I positioned Lloyd here for a reason."

Quanton watched him as he threw a piece of the croissant, he was eating to a tiny bird beside them.

"About the Lloyd thing…" Quanton began. "Do you think it's… ethical?"

"Ethical isn't the mission of this agency, Quanton."

"So, you think so too."

"We're talking about international safety here. I'll do whatever I must to save lives."

"He's just thirteen. And this whole legend of yours—"

"Not a legend, its history. I know you think it goes against your scientific standards, supposedly entering the realm of "magic" and what not, but what if the two are the same?"

Quanton drummed his fingers on the table. He still didn't know what to make of Cyrus's recent news.

"Ok, fine." He said. "Let's say its real. The curse was that the bloodline would be gone until someone worthy of wielding it came. How do we know Lloyd's the one?"

"I told you," Cyrus replied. "We ran tests. His blood definitely contains something other than human in it. I know no one could just believe what I have told you, but I have shown you proof! The ancient journal, the family line, even the water-sugar from Coated Coast! Where else do you think that could be from? You have reason to trust me!"

"Maybe I do. Maybe I believe everything you said is true, and that logically this is the best thing to do in this situation. I just have this doubt in the back of my mind screaming reason into my logic center. The journal containing that story could have been creative writing, based off real names, the water-sugar could have a possible explanation unfound as of yet. Maybe I just don't like putting a *kid's* life on the line." Cyrus sighed.

"Sometimes right and wrong just can't be a factor in the equation." Cyrus said. "Believe me, or don't. This man called Ezekiel believes in a human cleansing, and the rise of the cosmic age. And with the recent revival of those creatures he finally has the means to do it."

"But how does this man know of this if the blind spot was cast centuries ago?"

"I do not know everything about this," Cyrus said. "As much as I would like too. There are still some mysteries to solve and Lloyd will help us accomplish that."

"Lloyd," Quanton repeated. "What a lucky student. Not only does he get to participate in a term *not* set up by us, but he also has the weight of the world on his shoulders. And he didn't even have to volunteer."

"I know you like Lloyd." Cyrus said, a strange understanding in his voice.

"But this should turn out with no casualties, well, for kids anyway, if all goes according to plan. And remember, Karina isn't as ditzy as we told her to act like. Lloyd is well guarded."

A gentle breeze blew by, ruffling the leaves in a tree behind them. Quanton watched the tree for a second, then focused his attention back on Cyrus.

"I'm choosing to believe you," he said. "I will take any actions necessary to stop this global threat. But if anything happens to Lloyd, his mind or his blood is on your hands."

"That's all I needed to hear." Cyrus said, giving a firm nod. "Ezekiel plans to end the human era and re-arouse the cosmic one. Lloyd being a descendant of both humans and cosmics has inherited some of the mystic abilities the cosmics possess. Therefore, he should be able to communicate to the arising cosmics and withstand the cosmic energy Ezekiel is planning on gathering to end the humans. Hopefully winning the few cosmics on his side, he can get close enough to Ezekiel's mad schemes to disable the most threatening part about them. At that point Karina will contact us and we will arrive with our forces and put an end to Ezekiel for good. You understand the plan?"

"Crystal clear sir."

"The most important role you shall play is encouraging Lloyd. I've watched the way his mind works, and he may decide that he doesn't want a part in this sickening event as it escalates. That's when you, the closest to him of us all will do some coaching on for him. The words will come to you in the moment I'm sure."

"You've really got this figured out." Quanton said. "Excuse me sir if this seems disrespectful, but I mean no offense. Your strategy is to always have a carefully laid out plan, and if your people in the plan play their roles correctly, a nearly unbeatable one. For the most part it has worked. But I've watched when there's a disruption in your plans. You scramble for a solution, and it usually works out but very messily, as you are very reliant on your "master plan". Well assuming this is all reality, and the stakes are as high as they are, if this plan doesn't work, what will you do?"

"Well," Cyrus said, finishing his croissant. "In that case, God help us all, because the fate of the humans and the cosmics will be in the hands of a mad man."

CHAP5TER

They fired their guns at it, but the bullets bounced off its scaly hide. Lunging forward it tore into a man, killing him on the spot. Its black claws now glistening red, it turned around at the sound of a gunshot, and ripped the weapon from the man who held it. Defenseless the man tried to run, but to no avail. A purple hand plunged through his back, and out his chest before he slumped to the floor.

"Help!" a man screamed into his phone, hidden from the carnage behind a metal staircase. "It's got loose, and our weapons seem to have no effect against it!"

"It escaped!" Ezekiel roared from the other end. "What imbecile let it—"

"It broke through the glass sir. It seems to be fully developed now and stronger than ever, but please help us! We're dying by the handful out here!"

"I'm coming with the spasm ring." Ezekiel said, running from his evaluation on Alahn's cells. "Prevent it from leaving the compound at any cost."

"Hurry! I don't know how much longer I can—"

Ezekiel heard a crashing sound and screaming from the man he was talking to on his earpiece. A sound like liquid splattering followed, then nothing. Ezekiel burst through the doors leading to the room of the massacre, and saw the creature standing amongst a pile of fallen soldiers. Bullets that proved harmless against it were rapidly being fired its way. It got rid of the annoyance by slashing its arm through the air, sending a wave of purple aura towards the men that were firing at it. They slammed against a wall and slid to the ground. Ezekiel crept along the side of the wall, making sure to constantly stay behind it. More men were running into the room with better weapons, blasting the thing with every piece of ammo they had. Though bullets weren't lethal against it, they seemed to weaken it, as the creature now reacted slower and showed more pain when hit now. The creature formed a ball of pure kinetic energy in its hands and launched it at the group of soldiers guarding the door. Whether dead or knocked out, none of them got up. Stopping to search the room for more threats, the powerful beast gave Ezekiel enough time to sneak up behind it and clench the thick black ring he was carrying around its neck. It fell on its knees and held its head in its hands. If it had a mouth to scream from, cries of anguish would be heard coming from the creature.

"You've been a bad boy, test twenty-two." Ezekiel said, circling it. "Maybe you'll think twice before slaughtering my men after this." The creature bent backwards its head nearly touching the ground behind it.

"Doesn't feel good does it?" Ezekiel continued. "I'd imagine every muscle you have contracting is quite excruciating."

Too exhausted for consciousness, the creature slumped to the ground. Clicking a button on a mini handheld remote he possessed, Ezekiel turned off his spasm ring. His lackeys who had been hit by the kinetic energy ball, were coming to, and were slowly standing up.

"You there," Ezekiel said, pointing their way. He gestured to the dead bodies around them. "Clean up this mess. I'll get the creature to its stage two confinement."

Retrieving a long cart, Ezekiel put the unconscious beast onto it, and wheeled it down to a lower level of the compound. They passed by Alahn's containment room on the way, and the mutating scientist stood up from his cot.

"I heard the clamor." He shouted at Ezekiel. "Too bad you weren't better prepared for that, huh Ezekiel?"

Ignoring him Ezekiel continued on his way until reaching a door locked by a handprint recognition scanner. Placing his hand against the screen, the door emitted a beep, and opened. Inside was a small pool of water Ezekiel had collected from the Coated pond. He dumped his creation into it and watched as the water slowly began reviving it.

"Disobedient children are always trouble." Veronica said, coming up behind him.

"We're just lucky it was too young to have a real thought process." Ezekiel replied, locking up the door. "I must admit I did not expect it to grow so fast. This imprisonment it won't so easily escape."

"We must have lost half our fighting force to that thing." Veronica said. "First the meddling of Zahna, and now this. Setbacks are becoming too frequent around here."

"It is… invigorating." Ezekiel agreed. "But this was a good field test if nothing else. Soon the memories I fed it when it was young will kick in, and it will be more cooperative."

Looking through the small glass slit in the door, Ezekiel observed his creature, now rejuvenated assessing its new surroundings.

" Yes, our little created cosmic here will prove to be very useful in shaping a new world." He continued. "It won't be much longer now."

***   ***

Karina sat on the edge of her bed, not quite sure if she believed me. "Lloyd," she said, finally calling me by my real name. "You're saying a bed ridden old man is for some reason pretending to be against tattoos, but has them himself, and you think this makes him evil, why?"

Explaining things to Karina was unconventionally difficult.

"Maybe not full on evil," I replied. "But he somehow knew of a murder before it happened, or assumed it had already occurred, on top of the tattoo issue. Whether evil or not, he certainly knows something about what's going on here."

"And why do you need my help?"

"The maids at his house don't trust me anymore because of a false belief that I stole something of Mr. Richards'. Apparently, an expensive family heirloom went missing directly after I left. I'm not sure what that's about, but long story short, they won't let me near him, however you might be able to."

"How exactly?"

"Now that's the tricky part. You got any ideas?" Karina raised her hands in the air.

"I can't help you there." She said. "This mystery's up to you."

I looked out the window, thinking. How could Karina get close enough to Bard Richards to confront him? It would be difficult without breaking in, as the maids are probably on high alert after the incident with me. Well, the idea was the best one I could think of at the moment.

"We're going to break in." I told her, her face showing she wasn't exactly in favor of the plan. "His bedroom is on the second floor, to the backside of the house. You're going to knock on the door and keep the maids occupied while I sneak in from the back. If I remember correctly there's a second door that leads to the kitchen, and if you have the maids focused on you by the front door their backs will be right to me. I should be able to sneak up to his bedroom without issue."

"Ok..." she said, looking at the popcorn ceiling. "Loading that to memory files," she made a cranking motion with her hand beside her head. I was sure they gave me a childish "parental guardian" purposely. "But what if the kitchen door is locked?"

I took a gift card from my pocket.

"I don't carry this around for spending." I said. "Learned how to pick the locks with a card back in the second grade." "Great. But there's one flaw in this plan of yours." I raised an eyebrow at her.

"What happens if we get caught?"

"Well," I replied. "The police promised me a long stay at their headquarters if I have another slip up, so I suppose you would too." "No back up plan?"

"If you want to get caught go ahead." I said walking to the door. "But I'm not planning on it." I opened the door and held it for Karina.

"Come on. We've got a date with a geezer."

***   ***

"Hi!" Karina said excitedly as a maid opened the door. "Is this the water sugar factory? I've always wanted to visit this place! May I speak with you for a bit?"

"We had some trouble with the last person who was interested in this place." The maid replied. "Who are you?"

"Betty Wake." Karina said, using the fake name I gave her. "And I've heard all about the trouble you speak of. In fact I'm with the police. I'm a detective you see, trying to scope out your missing heirloom. I would like to speak with those who saw him. Is there anyone else here who I could talk to as well?"

"Rose!" the maid at the front door called out. "Could you come here a minute?"

"What," a second maid said, coming from the kitchen. "Who is this?" That was my cue. Running beside the black metal fence that surrounded the property until I got to the back of the house. Grabbing the top of the fence, I hoisted myself up, tucked my feet by my chest, and swung to the other side.

Ow. I thought, after landing on my side rather than my feet. *Gotta get better at that.*

Standing up and brushing the grass off of me, I continued to the back door. As suspected, the kitchen door was locked. I quickly performed the card trick any sensible person in this organization knew how to do and was able to unlock the door and get inside. Finding myself in the kitchen directly to the backs of the maids, I hastily, but carefully made it across the kitchen floor without any sound. I was less careful on the carpet, as the fluffy substance will absorb your footstep. Reaching the stairs, I climbed them on all fours. I had found that to minimize creaks on the stair boards, climbing them with your hands and your feet was a good idea. Once up the stairs I rounded the corner that led to Mr. Richards' room. The maids hadn't looked back at all and I had successfully reached my destination. I opened the door and stepped inside the windowless room I remembered from the day before. All was the same except for one factor; the bed was empty. Suddenly the door shut behind me and a firm hand was on my shoulder. Turning my head slightly there I saw Mr. Richards, out of bed and standing up straight.

"Welcome back boy," he said in that gruff voice of his. "What brings you here?"

I looked him up and down. His face certainly looked like an old man, but his legs and his arms looked like he was in his thirty's.

"Who are you?" I asked.

"Not who you thought I was." He replied. "Now, boy, I want you to know something." He moved his gripping hand from my shoulder onto the back of my neck. "I ain't crippled and I ain't old. You can't possibly overpower me, you hear? Call for help, make a move against me, this neck of yours is as good as snapped. Understand?"

The little nerves that were spreading down my legs and arms were creeping up into my stomach.

No time to be afraid. I reminded myself. *Worry beforehand. Do your job now.*

That was some advice our "on the field" teacher had told us back in school.

"Were you involved in that murder yesterday?" I asked another question.

"I was not holding the knife." he said. "But I knew of it, yes." "And you let it slip when I talked to you." I declared.

"Oh, that was not the murder I was referring to."

He led me to the small closet in the corner of the room. Opening it, he bent down, hand still on my neck, and ripped up a loose floorboard inside.

Underneath was black tarp, concealing something the size of a body.

"You killed him," I said. "You killed Mr. Richards and took his place."

"How perceptive."

He closed the closet door and tightened his grip around my neck.

"I knew," he continued. "After you barged in here and asked those strange questions, and possibly saw my tattoos, you were up to something. After I accidently let the murder answer slip, I knew you'd be back. I tried to scare you off by framing you for stealing that object, which is actually safely under my bed. But still I must be prepared, so I lay here, ready for you to come back."

"But how," I said. "How'd you know I was coming today at this moment?"

"Of course, I'm not alone in this caper. I've got scouts spying on you since you left. They alerted me once you were on the property." While we were talking, I had slipped my hand into my pocket. I grabbed hold and opened my pocketknife. It seemed like he was about to say something more, but he never got the chance. Whipping my little knife from my pocket, I slashed the arm of his hand that was holding my neck. He gave a surprised yelp of pain and let go of his hold. Not wasting a moment, I turned and slammed him against the wall beside his bed. I slid the knife to his throat.

"Now *I'm* in the position of power." I said. "You make a move against me and *your* throat will be the one in trouble."

"Oh, ho," he said back. From his voice you could hear that his arm was still hurt. "Congratulations. However," he took a mobile phone from his pocket.

On it he had a message ready to send. "You move that hand with your knife an inch and I send this to my boys outside. They get this, and your associate out there will have bullets through her skull before she could scream."

I stared him in the eyes. I thought a moment. And I didn't move my hand with my knife an inch. However, I did bring my left foot up into a kick and knocked the phone from his hand onto the ground.

Unfortunately, this gave him time to grab and twist my wrist in a very painful matter, forcing me to drop the knife. He then picked it up and pointed it at me.

"You're an impressive lad." He said. "But in the end, you're just a lad. And you're not going to beat the big boys like me." He bent down and retrieved his phone.

"Having such potential at a young age you could be a good asset." He continued. "The boss might like to meet you." *So, he has a superior.*

"On the other hand, your assistant there will not be the slightest bit of use, and there's always the witness issue…" He dangled his thumb over the phone.

"Don't do it." I said, an edge to my voice.

"Well, maybe since you asked so nicely…."

He pressed the send button on the shoot message.

"Oops." He said. "Guess I don't care about manners."

My first instinct was to look out a window to see Karina. My next was to run down and try to aid her. I could do neither of these things. A man was threatening me with my own knife in a windowless bedroom. I was absolutely helpless. I heard a couple of shots and some screaming outside.

"I'm sorry to say the maids will have to be shot as well." The false Mr. Richards said, walking back behind me, the firm grip on the back of my neck returning. "But you must understand no one can be allowed to tell the tale."

All I could do was stare at the ground. Karina's death was on me. The two maids' death was on me. I was foolish to think I could take a grown man in combat, and those three were the ones who had to pay for it. And now I was at the mercy of God knows who.

***   ***

Karina was running out of ideas for things to say to the maids. She kept looking over at the railing to see if Lloyd had returned yet. Currently she was in the middle of pretending to be a sketch artist. She nodded and said "hm mm" as the maids described him. She had never been much of a drawer, and her picture looked more like a cartoon character then a person.

"A question," the maid called Rose said. "But why do you need a picture?

Didn't you already take the boy in?"

"Um…" Karina thought fast. Or tried to. "Well he uh, escaped sort of, and we need to make sure we get the right kid."

"Escape?" the maid beside Rose asked. "Why, I was just at the police station answering questions and he was there. How on earth did he escape?" Karina looked up from her tiny sketch pad.

"It's actually a funny story…" Karina began, but Rose started to scream something.

"Oh my gosh, a gun!" she squealed.

Karina's training instantly kicked in and she dove for the ground as she heard the first shot fired.

"ROSE!" the now singular maid cried, before another shot was fired and she had a hole in her chest as well.

Karina regretted not being able to save them but had no time for guilt. She wasn't sure where the gunman or gunmen were and lying here out in the open wouldn't help her survive. Taking a chance, she dove for the door and somersaulted behind the wall. Bullets narrowly missed her and shattered the window in the kitchen. Karina stayed where she was for a moment and caught her breath. She allowed herself to wonder what was going on, but quickly pushed the thoughts away. She had been taught that thinking how to survive was top priority, not why her life was in danger. Suddenly a bullet crashed through the wall beside her, startling her to no end. The guns her attackers possessed had to be high caliber to crash through a wall like that. Deciding she needed to find better shelter, Karina made a run for behind the staircase. She made it and pressed her back flat against the wall. Her one advantage was that the gunmen couldn't see in the house, so she could hide for the time being. Her thoughts drifted to Lloyd. Was he alright? Was Mr. Richards crooked as he had said, and this was the cause of Lloyd confronting him? She had been briefed on how this term wasn't set up by her organization and that Lloyd was in actual danger. Karina had a horrible vantage point against the gunmen, and all she could do was stay in her hiding position and hope Lloyd was still alive.

***   ***

I was being directed through the hallway and then down the stairs by the man holding onto my neck behind me.

"This your first time being kidnapped?" he asked as we descended. "You're acting very mature about it."

I ignored him. I was reminded periodically of the knife that once belonged to me by a cold edge brushing my neck. We reached the bottom of the stairs, and hardly took a step further when out of nowhere a foot kicked my kidnapper across the face, followed by a leg to his stomach. His grasp against me slipped away and he stumbled back into the stair railing. A blonde woman rushed towards him and gave him a fierce jab to the left of his jaw and shot another to his right. She wrapped up the fight with her finishing blow of bringing his head down to her upcoming knee. The Mr. Richards imposter slid to the ground, unconscious. Before I could say a word to my savior, she grabbed me by my shirt and dragged me behind the wooden staircase.

"Ka-rina." I said, hiding my excitement that she was alive with mock irritation. "I had him right where I wanted him."

"Really?" she looked at me with an expression of amazement.

"Of course not." I replied. "I suppose we're hiding from the gunmen right now?"

"Brilliant Sherlock."

"Right. It's good to see you're not dead. What about the maids?"

"Gone. Both of them."

I ran my fingers through my hair.

"That's my fault."

"Lloyd, we could not have expected the man not to be bed ridden or have an army scouring the place."

"Yes, we could have. I underestimated him and overestimated myself."

"Well, you might be right."

"Thank you." I said, not sarcastically. "Now what if I told you that the cellar in this place was a better hiding spot than where we are now?"

"I'd agree, but the guys' guns can burst through the walls here. Even though we know where the cellar is, due to our research before coming here, I don't think we can make it without getting shot. Our movement could be easily followed through the windows throughout this place." I looked at the ceiling.

"Dang it." I said calmly.

I often dealt with my terror by being nonchalant. It usually helped calm me, and helped me think straight, but on some cases my brain would momentarily shut down. Now was one such time, and I could not come up with any brilliant ideas to get us out of this death trap.

"Karina," I said. "Any bright ideas? Surely they'll raid this place any minute now."

"I—" Karina began. "I think I can help. Would this qualify as dire enough to assist you on your term?"

"Karina we're going to die!"

"Right. Well... I got nothing."

"You got your combat training?"

"Uh... yes."

"Alright, listen. The fake Mr. Richards said they wouldn't kill me because I could be a "valuable asset" to whoever he was working for. So, I'm pretty safe for the moment. Before they storm the place get down on the ground and pretend to be dead. From there follow my lead."

"I'm trusting you Salt."

"That's all I ask for."

Karina got down on the ground and put herself in a deathlike position. I got on my knees above her, pretending to be distressed about her death. Now all we could do was wait for them to raid the house. I heard groaning from the other side of the staircase.

Oh, for gosh sake. I thought. *Just to make things worse.*

Thankfully before the awaking imposter could collect his thoughts and find us, the anticipated raid happened.

"Don't shoot!" I heard. "It's me you dolts. Put those guns down."

"Have you seen the boy or woman?"

"Of course, I did! Why do think I'm lying here on the floor? Help me up."

Alright Salt. I coached myself. *Time to put those acting skills everyone seems to think you have to good use.*

"Over here you killers!" I shouted.

They rounded the staircase. Besides the disguised man (who looked ridiculous still wearing his old man pajamas) there were three gunmen. "You shot her..." I said more quietly. "You shot her and killed her."

"Ohhh," whoever the man was behind the mask taunted. "Does the little boy miss his guardian angel?"

"Yeah. But you won't."

Karina suddenly sprung up and lunged at a gunman nearest to her, yanking his gun from his hands and taking out the next two with a few bullets. The man she stole the gun from went to attack her from behind her, but she was ready and drove the butt of her gun into his face, knocking him out. The whole time the man in the mask was just standing there, his hands raised above his head.

"Right then," I said. "The tides have changed once again. Now I suggest you take off that mask before my "guardian angel" shoots it off." Karina aimed the gun at him.

"No need to shoot." He said reaching for his mask. "You'll find I'm quite cooperative."

He took his mask off and revealed his face. He was much younger than he was posing to be, not possibly being over thirty. He had light brown hair, and some unkept sideburns.

"Okay." I continued. "I'll ask the question I asked once before. Who are you?"

"Hmmm." He said. "Good question. I've posed as so many people. Who am I really? Should I really say?"

"Yes, because we have a gun and you do not."

"Oh please. Like the "good guys" are going to do anything rash."

"Karina," I ordered. "In the arm."

Karina fired the gun and hit our captive in the higher part of his left arm. He howled in pain.

"Ow!" he loudly grunted. "You done pulverized my arm!"

"You want the other one meeting a bullet too?" I asked. "Cause it will. Real soon."

"Fine, fine!" he said, clutching his arm. "Michael Stane! That's who I am!

Now don't fire that blasted gun again!"

"What do you know about the murder that occurred yesterday?"

"Someone got too close to me." Michael Stane said. "Realized I wasn't my usual self. Had to take care of him."

"Who was he?"

"He went by the name Anderson."

I stared at him a moment and took a calming breath.

"He was a nice man." I said.

"What, you know him boy?"

"I was acquainted. Next question. Who do you work for, and where is he based?"

Michael was quiet.

"Well?"

"That's going too far. You're not getting that info from me."

"Karina, you got that gun ready?"

"Go ahead shoot me. See this tattoo?" he rolled up his sleeve to reveal the tattoo I had seen earlier. It was a picture of multiple planets that looked like earth, forming a symbol unfamiliar to me.

"This means total allegiance."

"We're gonna shoot."

"Go ahead."

There was silence for a moment.

"Gosh dang it!" I said. "Karina put the gun down. We're not shooting a helpless man."

Michael smiled.

"Yeah, grin." I told him. "You called our bluff. But you're not going anywhere. We got more than enough evidence against you. Let's see what the police have to say about this."

Before I left for the phone, I cuffed him across the face.

"And that's for framing me for stealing that heirloom and getting me arrested."

***   ***

I walked down the circular curved street of the Coated Coast town. I had someone to visit after the long day I had had. Someone had called the police having heard all the gunshots at the Mr. Richards home. Doug and Marcene arrived on scene and a lot of boring police developments followed. They were suspicious of me of course, but after investigating the house, finding the dead body, fingerprints, and what not, they had enough evidence to send Michael Stane and his three lackeys behind bars for a *long* time. Karina had said they were going to send him by train back to the city for his trial and imprisonment but first they were bringing him to the interrogation room. Hopefully they got more helpful information out of him then I did. The three gunmen were revealed to all have the same tattoo as Michael, so my term certainly wasn't over. There was some cult or group terrorizing this town, and I was going to put a stop to it. I came to the house I was going to. It was pale yellow just as he had said. I knocked on the door and it was answered by a middle age woman and a tiny dog.

"Hello dear." She said, obviously fighting back tears. "What brings you here?"

"I met your husband the other day." I said. "I just heard what happened today. I only came to say he seemed like a good man. And that I'm sorry about what happened."

"That's- that's sweet of you dear," she replied, trying her best not to break down. "He was a good man." She sniffled and wiped her eyes. "And I miss him."

She finally couldn't stand it anymore and broke down in a cry. I let her grieve for a moment, my eyes beginning to feel a bit watery.

"Thank you for coming to visit." She finally said, once she could manage it.

"No problem at all." I said. "It's getting late. I should be going. Goodbye Ma'am."

"Bye, dear."

I patted the dog on the head before I turned and left. I heard the door shut behind me as I walked into the night. This had to stop. Too many people had died already.

Whoever you are out there, I thought to myself. To the world. *Wherever you are, whatever you're doing, your days of victimizing this town are over.*

I'm Lloyd Salt, and I swear to it.

***   ***

"Still not talking Stane?" the interrogator circled Michael around the metal chair he was strapped too. "That tattoo means a lot to you."

"Are you seriously the best they had to offer?" Michael said. "Your interrogation tactics are that of an amateur."

"Oh, I haven't really started yet." The interrogator picked up a needle filled with a red liquid. "See this? Truth serum. You'll be highly responsive and honest. Amateur or not, my tactics along with this serum will do the job."

"Please." Michael said. "I can resist your petty serum. Or any torture methods you'll place on me."

"Now I'm not sure about that Mr. Stane." The interrogator walked closer with the needle. "The longer you last the more serious me and my tools will get."

He placed the truth serum injector on Michael's arm.

"I'd rather this to work, as it's not that I enjoy hurting people, but I don't mind it to get results."

He was about to inject the serum when a dart came shooting through the room and struck Michael Stane in the neck. Suddenly Michael began foaming at the mouth and the skin around his face tightened up. He made a few grunting sounds, then fell limp in the chair. Michael Stane was dead.

"Hey!" the interrogator cried as the man who had blown the dart fled the room. "Hey! Someone stop him!"

But when he entered the adjoining room all the police force was on the ground, alive but unconscious. Whoever had murdered Michael Stane, was gone.

CHAP**6**TER

Three Weeks Ago....

"Please," she said as she was directed into the police department's containment cell. "I swear I'm not working with the thieves! I'm totally against them!"

"Sure honey," an officer said, closing the cell. "We just found you in the Aquarium right when the alarm went off 'cause you were having a barbeque."

"Come on! I had nothing to do with the robbery!"

"Well what *were* you doing in the aquarium?"

"Preventing the robbery?" she said with a "duh" expression on her face.

"I don't think so."

"You gotta believe me!"

"How'd you know when it was happening then?"

"I—" she paused, contemplating what she would say. "I *was* working with them. Was as in past tense. I've rebelled against them now."

"That would still make you a criminal."

She sighed and sat on a bench in the cell.

"If you were working with them though," the officer said. "You might be able to get a certain extent of amnesty for telling us everything you know about them."

"I've only ever met them in one spot in town. I have no idea who they are, or where they're based. They just pay me to run certain errands for them."

"Errands such as?"

"I'm not going to admit to crime."

"So you are a criminal."

"Please just let me out. I can tell you more if you let me go."

"Sorry miss." The officer said. "Can't do that."

"Well," the girl replied. "I tried getting out the legal way."

She took a little ball from a secret pocket on the inside of her black jacket and rolled it outside of her cell. It opened and spun white clouds of gas into the room, momentarily blinding the officers.

"Hey, what's going on!?" a voice cried. "I can't see a thing!"

Making sure to hold her breath so as to not breathe in the gas, she took from a different pocket a skeleton key- a gift from her former associates. Getting it into the keyhole on the outside of her cell, she unlocked it and stepped out. Returning the key to her jacket pocket, she threw more of her gas bombs down continuing to blind the police officers as she ran. Soon she made it successfully out of the station and was off into the town.

Great. She thought as she continued to run. *Now I've no source of pay, and am wanted by the law, and probably the organization I was once a part of. Yup. Zahna Halland just has to live dangerously.* She decided that laying low in Coated Coast was her best option. Fingering the cash wad she had in her jeans pocket, she promised herself to live off that until another opportunity made itself clear.

***   ***

Closed due to unknown vandals. That's what the sign on the aquarium said.

Luckily, I didn't care much what the public was or wasn't allowed to do. I had a town to save, and I had to save it fast. Karina had made a point of sticking with me now that I was probably a target on our adversaries list. I had noticed Karina had gotten less annoying and immature after everything went down. Either my hunch about my organization instructing her to be a pain was right, or the seriousness of the situation had finally hit her. Either way didn't matter to me. Having a partner was more reassuring when dealing with frightening circumstances. It was early in the morning, just after breakfast and we were soon inside the aquarium despite what the sign said and had begun our search for any clues that could help us.

"It's dark in here." Karina said. "Would you like me to see if I can find out how to get the lights on?"

Since she was adamant that she could only offer minimal help, this being my term and all, she would not do a thing without me telling her so.

"Sure." I replied. "That'd be helpful."

She went off somewhere and I continued to look around. Without knowing what had been stolen it was quite hard to deduct what the reason was for the theft to target this place. I was quite sure everything was connected, and all had to do with whoever Michael Stane had worked for. The only thing now was locating him and find out why he was doing all this. Last night I had recalled that Michael, (while he was posing Mr. Richards) had requested to see Earl Alten. I had come to a conclusion from this that I would investigate later today. The lights flicked on and my eyes took a moment to adjust. Now seeing much more clearly, I took note how the tanks were void and empty of any water or animals. They must have shipped them all off after the robbery.

Also, that the sign had understated it. This was worse than being vandalized. It looked like a bomb had gone off in the place. There was debris and wreckage all over the floor, and water stains and broken glass coated it as well. Some tanks which must have been used for housing fish of some sort, were busted open too- probably the source of the glass and water. The hard part now was figuring out what was stolen. Knowing that may help us understand what goal this mystery man had. Karina soon returned to my side.

"Find anything worthwhile?" she asked.

"No." I said. "You?"

"Only the light switches."

"Did they tell you how to solve this mystery?"

"What? No."

"That's too bad."

Sarcasm was a good relief method for me as well.

"Come on," I said. "Let's explore a bit further."

We expanded our search into different rooms, and upper levels, but found nothing of use. We even tried looking in some "employees only" places but to no avail. We did find a storage room, which I guessed was the place stolen out of, for it had any goods an aquarium might need. What I couldn't figure out, was why some evil team needed aquarium supplies.

"This is useless." I complained. "We haven't found anything that could offer the least bit of information."

"Yeah, Lloyd," Karina said. "You've been very irritable and snappy ever since yesterday. This kind of attitude is not your usual way of communicating. It's not like yourself."

"Well, I do have two deaths on my conscience."

"Lloyd those maids were shot by the bad guys. You did not kill them."

"But it's my fault they—"

95

"Lloyd it isn't—"

"Of course, it is! It was my idea to take on Michael Stane without much foresight. It was me who tried to fight him rather than just let him take me.

Those two maids are dead because of my mistakes and there's no going back on that."

The room was silent for a moment.

"Lloyd," Karina said, understanding in her voice that I had never heard before. "I had no idea you felt so—"

"Well now you do." I replied. "Now let's get out of here and try to be the least bit useful. Why don't you be silent and let me brood for a while."

I was sure I would someday regret speaking to her like that. I had too many things on my mind to care now. We were just about to make our exit when a voice stopped us.

"Hey," it said. "I was going to remain hidden until you left, but I heard you mention taking on Michael Stane?"

A girl probably just under thirteen stepped into view from wherever she was hiding. She was gorgeous with long black hair, and white skin that complemented it. Her face was lightly freckled, and she was just on the medium between tall or short. I suddenly grew self-conscious and hoped she didn't think I was a jerk for the way I had spoken to Karina. "Um... yes we did." I said. "And you know him, how?"

"I've clashed with who he works with before." She replied. "I've heard his name spoken."

"And who are you?"

"My name's Zahna Halland." She held her hand out for me to shake it. "Who are you?"

"Lloyd Salt," I said shaking her hand. I hoped my hand didn't feel sweaty. "I um- am also against Michael Stane's compatriots."

For some reason I wished I could've held her hand longer. "Cool." She said. "I was just hanging out here. What are you doing?" Before I told her Karina butted in.

"You were just hanging out in a closed aquarium." Karina said skeptically.

"Right. How do we know you're not working with them?" Oh. Right. Beauty wasn't a free trust pass.

Come on Lloyd, I thought. *Get back in business mode. She's just a girl. Nothing special.*

"Karina's right." I said. "Explain yourself."

"Well clearly you've had a run in with the evil that's looming over this town.

Well so have I. Right here in this aquarium, actually. Bit of a scruff up I'm sure you can see" she gestured to the mess. "But oh well. At least the bomb helped me get away."

"You did this?" Karina asked.

"What would you do at gun point?" Zahna replied. "It was all self-defense."

"Why were they after you in the first place?" Karina clearly did not trust her.

And you shouldn't either, Salt.

"Whoa," Zahna said. "When did this turn into interrogation? Maybe I should have stayed in hiding."

"What my associate is wondering," I said. "Is why you are here, how this mess got made, and why you revealed yourself to us. Answer those and we'll see if we believe you from there."

"Easy." Zahna answered. "Hiding from my enemies. Used a bomb a couple weeks before, to escape my enemies. And we both have the same enemies. This all revolves around my enemies if you couldn't tell. Now it looked like you needed some help. Could I assist?"

"First," Karina said. "Give us more detail on what went down here."

Zahna looked at her exasperated.

"All you people do is ask questions." She said. "If you must know, I was trying to stop the robbery from happening. I failed, as you can see, and they got away with the supplies they needed. Despite the mini explosion I caused. We all cleared up?"

Karina looked at me.

"Salt," Karina said. "Do think we can trust her?"

"Her story lines up," I noted. "But of course, we have no proof. Hey, you said they got off with some supplies, right?" "Yes?" Zahna said.

"Do you happen to know what it was they stole? It would help us out quite a bit."

"As far as I know..." Zahna replied. "They made off with some big containment tanks with the really strong glass stuff that this place was going to use for octopus, and advanced water test tubes. But that's all I know of course. They could've snagged more."

"It makes no sense." I said. "What use would a crime cult thing have for stuff like that?"

Zahna looked like she was debating something.

"Are you guys detectives or something?" she asked.

"Or something." I answered.

"Right, well... you want to stop these guys, right?"

"Of course."

"So, I can trust you with something they absolutely can't find out about?"

"You have my word."

"Great. Then follow me."

She went off into the aquarium, and I began following her.

"Lloyd," Karina whispered to me. "Something seems off about her. She seemed too eager to greet us don't you think? And much too casual about all this."

"So far she's given us the only lead we have on this whole aquarium subject." I said. "We'll have to trust her for now."

"Just so you know," Karina continued. "I saw how you blushed when you shook hands."

"I did not."

"And you said "um" like three times. You usually sound like you're in a business meeting."

"Karina, stop. She caught me off guard okay?"

"Her, and her looks?"

"Shut up."

Soon Zahna stopped and opened a door beside her.

"In here." She said.

We followed her into small a room which was for the most part empty, with random strewn supplies, and a table in the center. Atop the table was a large fish tank filled with water and housing a creature I had never seen before.

"What is that?" I said in wonder, looking closer at the tank.

"As far as I can tell," Zahna said. "The whole reason for all the incidents around here. The disappearance, this robbery, and just recently that murder, all connect to them getting ahold of a creature like this."

"How'd you get one?"

"With the help of these guys," Zahna said, showing me a handful of metal balls. "I was able to stall them long enough before the police got here for them to make a choice: retrieve their precious cargo or make out with the items they stole. They chose to leave this behind. Why they had it here in the first place I'm still figuring out."

"What were the metal balls you showed me?"

"Different types of smoke bombs. One was flammable and exploded when it got shot, creating the wreck outside."

"Ah. But you didn't tell me one thing about them." I said, preparing to make an accusation. "They were given to you by the evil organization we're tailing.

So, what's this? A trap?"

"How'd you—"Zahna began.

"The tiny picture on the balls," I replied. "Earths shaped in an infinity symbol. That's their logo."

"I swear I don't work for them. I—"

"That's hard to believe miss Halland. Now you're going to tell us why you brought us here."

She looked at me and Karina.

"Guys, just hear me out, —"

"You've got five minutes."

"I used to work with them, okay? I was desperate for money, and they paid me to do little jobs for them that would save them time. I- I know I did some illegal things, but I'm trying to make that right by thwarting as much of their schemes as I can! That's why I was at this aquarium!"

"It seems you have failed so far. Why were you desperate for money?" She stopped for a moment.

"Man, you guys are getting personal." She said.

"Get on with it." Karina egged.

"Look, my father left my mother shortly before she died of cancer. I was shipped off here to live with my batty, dirt poor aunt. I just got sick of it you know? Having next to nothing. I just felt I didn't deserve it. Happened to run into them while they were doing a job. Offered me a payroll to help them out when they contacted me. These sweet smoke bombs were a memento from them. After a while they turned on me. Decided I knew too much. Luckily, I escaped, with the help of the smoke bombs they gave me. Failed at stopping them here and have been hiding out in this place ever since. My aunt is probably worried sick, but I expect they know where I live."

"Aaaannd," I said. "Times up." "So?" Zahna said.

"It's a good story." I replied. "Unfortunately, none of it is verifiable."

"Actually," Zahna said. "I could go take you to my aunt." Before I could respond, Karina spoke.

"Lloyd," she said. "Come look at this."

I joined her as she was looking into the glass tank. The little creature inside it was glowing vibrant blue, coloring the water around it. Whatever was inside the tank was unlike anything I had ever seen before. It resembled a large salamander, but with more distinct features and strong limbs. At the end of its arm and leg appendages were little black things that looked like claws. It was covered head to toe with strong looking scales, colored purple. On its face were deep black eyes, and small pointed ears. The glowing stopped and seemed as if it just grew a couple centimeters.

"What is it doing?" I asked.

"My best guess is eating." Zahna said. "I was afraid it would die because I didn't know what to feed it. It does this and grows each time, and I haven't fed it anything."

"Incredible." I said. "It's like, absorbing nutrients from the water. Does it grow like that every time?"

Zahna nodded.

"Now I'm afraid it'll die because it'll outgrow its tank." She said.

"If it means so much to these people we're after, why haven't they come back for it?" I wondered.

"I don't know everything." Zahna said. "You ask me like I know inside out about these guys."

"It's clearly not fully grown." Karina noted. "I wonder how big it'll get. Maybe they're waiting for it to grow?"

"Or," I said. "Or, they already have what they need, and aren't risking coming back to get it."

"That would still leave the question of why they brought it here in the first place." Zahna said.

"That is strange," I agreed. "What is the reasoning behind that?"

103

Suddenly Karina fell to the ground, shaking like electricity was coursing through her body. I noticed a metal cable around her ankle, probably the source of the problem.

"Go for the dangerous one," said a female voice from behind, for the second time that day. "And the rest fall like leaves from a tree. Never fails."

A woman dressed in black workout pants, and a thin purple jacket was standing before us. She was a slim brunette with her hair in a ponytail.

"Yeah well," I said, taking what Zahna was offering me behind her back.

"There's a first for everything. Zahna, now!"

Zahna went to throw one of her smoke bombs, but with impressive speed and agility, the woman caught it.

"Please," she said. "Like we haven't adapted to your tricks by now, girl."

"Why are you coming back now," Zahna asked. "Why not before?"

"My dear," the woman said in a menacing way. "It kept you in this place did it not? I notice you have not interfered with us since you found it."

"So..." Zahna said, figuring it out. "My keeping tabs on it was your plan all along! It distracted me from what I should have been watching."

"Bingo." Purple jacket lady said, advancing on us. "And now it has put all our most prominent problems together. How exciting. And without your guardian angel," she motioned to Karina, unconscious on the ground. "You don't stand a chance."

"What, was that her high school nickname or something?" I said doing a dramatic shrug. While my hands were up, I threw the gas bombs Zahna had secretly handed me, grabbed Zahna by the hand and ran out of the room. The lady in there hadn't been so wise to hold her breath. She would be hacking for quite some time.

We continued to run out of the aquarium as fast as our legs would allow.

"Are we going to just leave your girlfriend back there?" Zahna asked as we ran.

"Unless you have some shockingly brilliant plan to get her out. And she's not my girlfriend by the way. I'm single. Well, not that It matters you, I was just noting that—"

I stopped myself before I could say anything else stupid and changed the subject.

"Be prepared in case they've got back up outside," I said, handing back her smoke bombs. "You probably know how to use these better than me."

We burst out the aquarium doors, and kept on running, not waiting to see if anyone else was on the premises. We were lucky that day. We escaped the bad guys through their underestimation. Of course, that could only work so many times. I had already used it twice.

"Where too?" Zahna asked.

"Man, I don't know!" I said through deep breaths. "I just avoided a death scenario for the second time in two days! I'm getting a little overwhelmed."

"Where's somewhere safe?"

I thought a moment. Going back to the hotel would be foolish; it probably had eyes on it everywhere. Going to Zahna's aunts wouldn't work; that was probably being monitored too. But there was one place with someone I sort of knew that *probably* was safe.

"We're going to the faded yellow house next to the supermarket," I said.

"I've got someone there who might invite us to stay."

"I'm going to trust you, Lloyd."

And once again I said: "That's all I ask."

***   ***

We arrived at the yellow house flustered, and out of breath. We hadn't stopped running the whole way for fear the woman would catch up with us.

Knocking on the door, Anderson's wife soon answered it.

"Oh, it's you again." She said looking at me, and then Zahna. "And you've brought a friend this time."

"Yes," I said, "but unfortunately I'm not here for a visit today. You know how some people killed your husband?"

"Those horrible, persons" she had a sad look in her eyes. "Yes, I do."

"They're after us now, and we need somewhere to hide."

"They're after—" she looked at us in disbelief. "But you're just children!"

"They don't care." I said. "Please let us in before they find us."

She did, and we were soon settled on her sofa, and due to her demanding, we explained everything that had happened. We left out the bit about the creature we had discovered, and how Karina was kidnapped, just to not complicate things too much for Ms. Ross. That was her name I had found out.

"Simply insane." Ms. Ross said, when we were finished. "They killed my husband because they thought he was figuring out their ruse with Mr. Richards, and they're after you because you called them out on it?" "Basically." I replied.

"Oh, my," she said. "Oh my. I never knew the crime wave was this bad."

"We're all figuring it out as we go." I said. "And don't tell *anyone* we're here.

We wouldn't want them finding out and making you a target."

"Of course," she said. "Do your parents know about this."

"Neither of our parents are in town." Zahna said, from next to me on the couch. "We're on our own."

"Well," Ms. Ross said, standing from her rocking chair. "This is all a lot to take in. Cooking calms me a bit. I'll be in the kitchen fixing some lunch if you need me."

After she left, Zahna and I took the opportunity to discuss the more complex events going on.

"So, they've got Karina," I said. "Our living places are most likely compromised, and they've retrieved that creature thing in the tank. We are pretty screwed."

"Mm," Zahna agreed. "I'm not sure what to do from here." I considered a thought that formed in my head.

"Well," I said, "we could begin by expanding our little team here."

"Who do you have in mind?"

"Earl Alten."

***   ***

Karina came to groggily. Every muscle in her body felt like it was on fire. As her vision cleared, she could see that she was in a small, windowless room.

The ground was cement, and the walls were made of hard gray material. The room had no furnishings whatsoever, and the only thing in it was her.

Standing up, Karina pounded on the metal door that led into her room.

"Hey!" she shouted. "Anybody home?"

She pounded some more. Soon a hatch on the top of the door was lifted, and she could see the face of the woman who had shot her ankle through the box hole.

"Are you always so cranky when you first wake up?" the woman asked.

"Where's Lloyd," Karina asked. "Did you get him too?"

"Unfortunately, he and that girl escaped." The woman replied. "We did not expect for him to have the smoke bombs as well." Karina smiled.

"You can't even catch a thirteen-year-old." She said.

"Oh, we will. This time though, we'll let him come to us. When it's on our terms we never lose."

"Who are you?"

"They call me Veronica. But you can call me whatever you like."

"How's about dirt bag?" Karina said.

"I'll take it." Veronica said. "Now how's about you tell me who you're working for, and how they know about us."

"Like I would."

"Maybe not now. But once we get a hold of that Lloyd of yours, you may be more cooperative"

"You won't get Lloyd. He's too smart."

"Oh, but that's just it. We'll make it appear he's outsmarted us in every way. But in reality," Veronica showed Karina the palm of her hand and slowly clenched it into a fist. "He'll be walking right into our hands." Karina just glared at her.

"Well, I'm off." Veronica said, getting ready to close the hatch. "Let us know when you're about to die of hunger, we'll figure something out. Is there anything you would like me to say to the big man on your behalf?"

"Yeah," Karina said. "Tell him to go, to, Hell." Veronica grinned. "I guess one can dream." She said.

The hatch was shut, and Karina was left alone, in her solitary confinement.

CHAP**7**TER

"How does it feel?" Ezekiel asked the now unrecognizable Alahn. His transformation from human to cosmic was now as complete as it could be. Alahn was entirely covered in purple scales, and his fingernails had grown into black claws. His hair and mouth were gone, and he now communicated by telepathy like a true cosmic. His toes had merged together like a cosmic's and he was slowly developing some of their mystic powers.

"How does it feel to be out of your human manifestation and a part of something greater?"

"You've changed me." The thought was forced into Ezekiel's head. Telepathy. *"But I will always be human."*

"And you say that as if you want to be human." Ezekiel said. "You say it as though being a human is great. How could you possibly think that?"

"I've figured it out. What you're up to. The reason for all of this."

"Well a gold star for you. Tell me, do you approve?"

"I would never approve of genocide, you mad man! And converting yourself to a cosmic? Its trans-species is what it is, absolutely absurd and wrong."

"It seemed to work on you, Alahn. And I don't just plan to do it on myself. All my people, who all have wisely chosen to follow me will be transformed as well. Into something better than human. You see, when I end the human age, what you call trans-species will be Noah's ark, and I shall be Noah."

"This is not right Ezekiel. Look at all you have done already. Killed baby creatures in order to extract their cells to create your little monster. Murdered innocent people. Took away even my humanity. You're insane."

"I'm insane?!" Ezekiel roared, pounding the glass that separated them. "This earth has had years of sickness, war, sadness, and pain! All you humans offer it is sin, and you have contaminated the entire planet with it. I offer to cleanse all that, create a paradise, and you call me insane?!"

Ezekiel took a breath and calmed down. He was known for outbursts when the talk got philosophical. Silence fell between the two, tenseness in the air.

"I feel the other cosmic." Alahn put into Ezekiel's thoughts. *"It's not yet wise enough for words but I feel its emotions. It feels alone, and*

scared. It doesn't understand what it is, or even why it is. How could you do that to a living creature, one that you want to rule the world?"

"It is not yet sentient." Ezekiel replied. "But soon what you helped me put into its head will be unearthed."

"What you had me do to its brain. We were programming its mind?"

"Not programming but setting a base for all its other thoughts. Certain memories and beliefs will be flooding into it any day now."

"So, it's finished then. All you have to do now is wait and your mission will be accomplished."

"Yes. Death to the humans, and long live the cosmics. But there is something I must know, the reason why I came to speak with you. You can reach out and feel the other cosmic's presence, as can all cosmics. They are all tied together through their cosmic powers. But do you feel others? Can you feel any other cosmics out there in the universe?"

"I haven't tried."

"Well today you will."

Alahn looked up at the ceiling.

"Ok. Here goes."

Alahn reached out, searching the universe for others with the cosmic blood. Of course, he felt the other one in the compound, but were there anymore? Yes. A baby one, also in the compound, the one Veronica just retrieved from the aquarium. Alahn needed to reach further, outside the compound. He felt for any being holding the cosmic blood, on earth or in the universe. He felt one, another in coated coast, but… off somehow. Far away in a pocket of the Atlantic Ocean he felt many, a whole group. So, there were more on earth. He tried to sense outside of earth's boundaries into the outer reaches of the universe, but he found… nothing.

"There are more on earth." Alahn told Ezekiel. *"Out in the Atlantic Ocean. A whole colony of them."*

"So, they did seed another area." Ezekiel said. "No matter. Soon the whole earth will be their domain. And what about outside of earth?"

"I felt nothing. No traces of cosmics." Ezekiel looked pained.

"I knew it." He said. "I knew this would happen. Those idiots! Earth was the only thing safeguarding us, and then they just abandoned it!"

"What do you speak of? Why did you say "us"?"

"I was once a part of the cosmics." Ezekiel said. "I once had their blood. But they stripped me of it. They took everything away from me. But I realized… it was not them who did this to me. It was humanity. They were the fault behind my suffering. Earth… it was shielding us from those that hunted us. Its unique atmosphere kept our scent from them. But they were gone too long, the way their scales absorbed the atmosphere wore off, and they were found, and massacred. The cosmics here on earth are the last of their kind."

"Who was hunting you?"

"The Others."

"Who are the—"

"You know too much already." Ezekiel turned and left. "And don't you try to communicate with the other cosmic. There will be consequences."

And with that he was gone. Alahn didn't understand everything he had said, but he did know a few things. Ezekiel wished to make the humans extinct and have the cosmics dominate the world. He had merged his cells with cosmics to see how the human body would react. Since it was successful, he would transform himself and his followers into cosmics, like he had Alahn become to survive the human cleansing. He had not told Ezekiel about the other cosmic blood he had sensed in Coated Coast. He had figured out what was off about that one. Whoever it was, it was part *human.* And with what Ezekiel had planned for the world, that may be the last bit of resistance the humans had.

***   ***

We were careful and stealthy on our way to the cabin by the pond. Not wanting to be out in the open for long, Zahna and I were constantly ducking behind things, and hurrying across streets. Luckily, we got to our destination without any disturbance.

"In there," I said, pointing to the wooden cabin once we were next to the pond. "That's where he's living."

"And why do you think he can help us?" Zahna asked.

"I'm sure he's here looking for his missing father. He may know some things we don't. And we're going up against an evil society. We'll need all the hands we can get."

"Right. Well, after you."

I looked at Zahna. She was the most beautiful girl I had ever met and was often distracting from the mission. Like now for instance. I got my head out of the clouds and approached the cabin. Opening the door there was a yelp from the inside as a startled boy stood to his feet. He had short cropped brown hair, with moles dotted around his face. He was dressed in blue jeans and a button up shirt and judging from his looks I guessed he was fourteen or fifteen.

"Whoa," he said. "Um, I was not expecting company, I uh was just hanging out here and..."

"Earl Alten," I said. "I'm Lloyd Salt, and I think I can help you find your father."

"Wait," Earl said. "How do you know my name? I..." he seemed to forget about what he was previously saying. "Did you say you could help find my father?"

"Yes, but we could use your help."

"We? But you're—" Earl seemed to notice Zahna for the first time. "Oh, um, well of course. Anything you need. I'm glad to see someone still cares about my father."

"All right," I began. "You may want to sit down. I should probably explain to you what's going on."

I told him of the run in with Michael Stane who was posing as Mr. Richards, and how we were attacked at the aquarium and Karina was kidnapped. I also explained about the creature we had found in the tank. When we were done, I expected Earl to question my reliability, but he seemed very understanding. "That would explain why they took him." he said when I was finished. "He was a renowned biologist. If they're harboring some sort of creature like you say, my father's expertise would come in handy. Um... do you think he's still alive?"

"We gotta hope so." I said. "He's been on the inside for a while. If we can spring him, he'll have invaluable information."

"I've been at this for a while." Earl said. "My mom thinks I took the train to a two-week summer camp, and I've already used up eight days. At this point I'll do nearly anything to get my father back."

"Good." I replied. "This will probably get real dangerous."

Real dangerous. *Real* danger. I always suspected my organization set up the terms, but made the situation *feel* real and dangerous. But this was certainly real. People were dying. And they sent a kid to stop it? Wasn't that unethical and absurd?

But they always taught us to think of ethics last. I thought. *They believe that philosophy more than I thought.*

I had disagreements with how my organization dealt with things from time to time, but this really made me question their tactics. Suddenly a dizzying feeling came over me. I felt very warm and woozy, and my vision was going blurry.

"Can you hear me?" A voice inside my head said. *"Can you feel me?"*
It was as though I was thinking these things, but *I was not.* They were being forced into my head somehow. My sight was slowly becoming even more clouded over.

"Who are you?" I asked. "Where are you?"

I thought I heard someone saying something to, me but my hearing had become all muffled as well. There was no response from the voice.

"Hello?" I said.

"Can you hear me?" Echoed around my head again.

"Yes! I—"

Wait, that's it! If the voice is "thinking" to me, maybe I have to "think" to it! I thought, deliberately this time.

"Yes, of course." It said. *"What else? Would you talk to thin air? Wait, have you not done this before?"*

"No of course not, nothing like it."

"So you don't know. Interesting."

"Know what?"

This was just getting more confusing. I could now hear nothing, and I was actually blacking out.

"You really have no idea, do you?" The voice continued. *"This will be a bit harder than I thought."*

Everything was dark. Besides the voice in my head I was deaf, and now I was blind.

"What's going on?" I asked. *"What's happening to me?"*

"Focus. Make your goal to communicate with me. I can see you. Can you see me?"

"No, I can't see anything."

"Concentrate on one thing. Direct all your thoughts to having this conversation with me."

I did the best I could, considering I had never done it before.

"Nothing's happening." I thought.

"Imagine there's energy flowing through you." It replied. *"Channel that energy to seeing me."*

I had no idea how to channel imaginary energy.

"I'm sorry," I started. *"I can't—"*

"Oh no, someone's coming. I gotta go. I can't let them see me doing this."

"Wait! I need to know, who are you?"

"Alahn Alten. We'll speak again."

Suddenly I was back in the real word. With all my senses returning simultaneously, it was nearly too much for me to bear. The sunlight seemed to be frying my eyes, and the noises around appeared amplified by a microphone.

"Ohhh," I groaned, not feeling so well.

I backed up and slammed into a wall.

"Lloyd!" Zahna said. "Are you okay? You haven't been responding to us."

119

"I—" I was still adjusting to everything. My vision was back to normal now, and besides an earache my hearing was fine as well. "I- I've been somewhere else."

"What are you talking about?" Earl asked. "You've been standing here blankly this whole time."

"My body was here. *I* was somewhere else."

"That makes no sense." Zahna said.

"I was talking to someone," I continued. The realization of who I was talking to was still setting in.

"Yeah, we heard you say a couple things." Said Earl. "But who- how were you talking to someone?"

"Earl," I said, looking towards him. "I was speaking to your father."

Earl looked at me, scrunching his face a little.

"You can't be serious." He said.

"No, really. I was in this void, and we were conversing through my thoughts. He said he could see me, but I couldn't see him. Kept telling me to channel this imaginary energy so I could see him." Zahna and Earl shared a look of concern.

"Lloyd," Zahna said, slowly. "Are you sure this *actually* happened?"

"Yes!" I said. "I—" A wave of awfulness ran through my body. "I don't feel so well."

The worried looks of Zahna and Earl was the last thing I remembered before I fell to the ground, and everything went black.

***   ***

My first waking thought was jealousy that Earl had spent so much time with Zahna without my presence. The two sat together discussing things that Earl had in his notebooks. With no sense of time and no idea how long I had been out, I was actually quite thankful they had left me where I fell, so I knew where I was. Standing up, I slowly and shakily approached Zahna and Earl.

"Sorry about that." I said. "Just needed a power nap."

"Oh, right." Earl said, rolling his eyes. "Dude, we've been worried about you." "How long have I been out?" I asked.

"A few hours." Said Zahna. "The sun is going down."

"We've been here for that long!?"

"Where else would we go with a sleeping kid?" Earl said.

"True. I just don't like being in the same place for long. Gives us more of a chance to be found."

I looked at the couple of notebooks sprawled on the floor.

"So, what've you guys been up too?" I said, beckoning towards the notebooks.

"Earl has cataloged all his findings during his stay in this town." Zahna explained. "We were going through them to see what we could piece together."

I sat down next to Zahna.

"Good to see you've been working." I said. "Um, about what I said earlier, I know it sounds impossible, but I'm telling the truth. Maybe-"

"I believe you." Said Earl. "I've uh... seen something "impossible" as well.

What you said isn't any more farfetched then what I have to say."

"And what is that?" I asked.

"So, remember when we were at the aquarium this morning," Zahna started. "And we saw the water tank glow, we were speculating that was how the animal we saw ate?"

"Yes."

"Earl says that since he's been staying here, early each morning, and late each night, the entire pond glows just like how we saw." I raised an eyebrow.

"Soo," I said. "We think there are more animals like the one in the aquarium living in this lake?"

"That's what we've come to." Earl said.

"Do you think this all has to do with the water-sugar?"

"Could be." Zahna said. "Perhaps that's what they're eating when they glow like that."

"But the water-sugar ran out." I reminded them. "They can't be eating it anymore."

"That's true." Said Earl. "And uh, there's another variable to this that I haven't gotten to yet. Whenever the water glows it's just for very briefly, which is probably why no one has noticed it yet, but one night I got curious about what would happen if I dropped something in it when it glowed. I stayed by the pond one night until it glowed again and dropped a small rock in it." "And what happened?" Zahna asked. "It... just disintegrated." Continued Earl. "The rock touched the water, and like, burnt up."

I stood up and looked out the cabin window at the pond. Everything about this was just getting more confusing. The sun was setting casting an orange reflection over the water. It was beautiful.

"Why don't we go out and wait by the pond," I suggested. "I want to see this thing glow.

"It's almost night." Earl agreed. He stood and opened the door. "Come on out, and I'll show you."

***   ***

As we were waiting beside the pond, we discussed my strange encounter with Alahn.

"It was pitch black, and silent," I was saying. "I couldn't hear anything but the voice that was talking to me. He kept trying to coach me, get me to see him, or something. He had to stop because he said someone was coming... when I asked who he was he said: Alahn Alten."

"So he's alive." Earl said. "That's relieving. But how could he communicate with you? He's a scientist not a wizard."

"I don't know much more than you do." I said. "All of this is quite the mystery."

"Maybe we should put everything we know out right now." Zahna said. "Sort of like a clue check."

"Why not?" I began. "I'll start. Feel free to add whenever you like."

I picked up a stick beside me and drew a box in the dirt. I labeled it: Day One.

"I arrived here, and began canvassing the town, learning whatever I could. After speaking with Mr. Richards, A.K.A Michael Stane, he framed me of thievery to scare me off. Then some associates of his killed Anderson because he was growing suspicious."

I drew another box labeled: Day Two.

"Returning to his mansion, this time with Karina, we managed to take him down and learn most of his scheme. I've worked it out that he posed as Mr. Richards to make sure the townsfolk weren't onto anything, while at the same time luring in Earl, so they could use him as leverage against his father." "Why do you figure that?" Earl asked. "He sent for you. Actually, I pretended to be you to get inside."

"So," Earl continued. "What we gather from this, is they want something of my father, and they also know I'm here."

"Exactly."

Picking up the stick once again, I drew another square, this time labeling it: Day Three.

"Today Karina and I got up early to visit the robbed aquarium. There we met Zahna and found the strange animal inside the tank. We were ambushed and our attacker revealed that they purposefully left the tank to distract Zahna and keep her in one place."

Zahna nodded. The night air was becoming cooler, and I shivered as a soft wind blew.

"We managed to escape, but Karina was taken. Since then we found a safe house and came and met you." I pointed to Earl.

"Where shortly after I made mental contact with your father, and fainted, probably because of the strain telepathy was putting on my mind." I looked up at the sky and exhaled.

"What can we learn from that?"

By now the stars were out, and the moon was shining.

"I'll add something to the pot, if you don't mind." Earl said. "It may help you guys if you know exactly in what my father specialized in. He mostly researched and worked on the way cells worked together, learning how to stitch them into different things and sorts. With this kind of work, he also dabbled a bit in cloning."

After Earl's statement, I thought for a moment.

"I've got a crazy idea." I said.

"It's better than no idea." Zahna replied. "Shoot."

"What if they're trying to create more of that thing we saw at the aquarium?

And that's why they need Earl's dad, to use his genius in that field?"

"But, why?" Earl said. "Why would they need to create one, if they had that one in the tank, and possibly in this pond?"

"I have a couple theories on that," I continued. "First, is that the environment is no longer compatible for them to grow into an adult, which for some reason they need, so they have to create one in controlled surroundings."

Earl and Zahna's facial expressions didn't bash it but didn't say: "Yes that's it!" either.

" My next guess gets a bit more science fictiony." I looked at Earl to ask him a question. "You said your dad dabbled in cloning, right?"

"Correct." He said.

"Could they maybe give specific memories to the clones, or like, program their minds with a certain thought process?"

"To a clone?" Earl looked like he was trying to remember something. "Well, I'm sure they *could*. From the way my dad explains it, clones are a bit of a blank slate. If you fed its mind memories and thoughts while it was developing, you could set a background for it."

"Then that's what they could be doing." I said. "Making its mind to their liking, so when its full grown it'll be under their control."

"They could turn it into a weapon." Zahna noted.

"Exactly. And with this undiscovered creature, who knows what kind of power it has? It could possess capabilities that we never thought possible... "Like telepathy." Zahna said, catching on.

"Like telepathy." I replied.

"So wait," Earl began. "You're saying my father could be learning the ways of these new beings while creating them?"

"Possibly." I said. "Now we have one advantage; they probably don't know we've figured out all this, or that I can talk to Alahn. We could really use this. However, as my organization has taught me, never suspect you're a step ahead. That's usually what your opponents want you to think. Rather assume that you're a step behind, so you will always over prepare, and ensure victory."

My two associates nodded. I hardly considered them acquaintances yet, and they would have to work to earn the title "friend".

"This is a lot to take in." Earl said, lying down in the grass.

"Yes, it is." I agreed. "Yes, it is."

Sometime later it happened. The night was in full force, and just as I was beginning to get tired, the pond started glowing. It was beautiful, and mysterious. Dim blue light resonated around the whole pond, bright in the center, thinning out by the edge. Earl, who had waited at the brink of the pond to demonstrate how it would eat up any object he put in it, dipped a large rock onto the surface. Just as Earl had described, something like a blue flame ran up the whole rock, incinerating every bit of it, until nothing was left in Earl's hand. It all happened very fast, the entire event spanning across no more than five seconds, and the pond reverted to normal.

"Incredible." I said.

"It does that twice a day." Earl said. "I can't explain it."

"The same thing happened in the tank at the aquarium." Zahna said.

"It must be related to those creatures somehow." I yawned.

"Well, I think it's time to turn in." I said. "We'll show you to our "safe house" Earl."

"Great," Said Earl. "Let me just grab some of my things."

We were about to leave when a wave of vertigo washed over me.

"G-guys," I stammered, feeling weak. "It- it's happening again, I—"

Suddenly I could talk no more. Once again, my vision blurred, and my hearing muffled. I was back in that dark void, deprived of sight and sound.

"Alahn," I thought, prepared this time. "Is that you?"

"Yes." Alahn's voice was forced into my thoughts. "Getting better at this are we?"

"I was ready this time. I'm Lloyd, by the way. Lloyd Salt."

"Lloyd Salt. Catchy name. Listen. By now you must know something beyond human capabilities is taking place."

"I've about figured that out. Earl Alten is your son, correct?"

"Yes, he is. Why?"

"Don't worry. He's safe. He's with us."

"He's with you?" Alahn said, sounding startled. "They've got tabs on him! He will endanger you and anyone that includes "us"!"

"I've thought of that." I replied. "I'm willing to take the risk."

"Listen. You need to know something. You're not ordinary. Your blood... it has cosmic D.N.A. mixed in with it. "

"Whoa, whoa, what are you saying?"

"You are somehow connected to the cosmics, a race that once lived amongst humans."

"Cosmics... what are they? What do you mean I'm connected?"

128

"I'll explain, but I can't from here. You need to connect us. It has to be a two-way connection."

"You're trying to get me to see you again?"

"Yes. Focus. Create a bridge connecting both of us."

"I'll try. No promises."

And I did try. Nothing happened. How could I connect me to him? I didn't have the capabilities he did... or did I? He said I was "connected to the cosmics". Could that mean I possessed the power he did, and that's why he could communicate with me? This time with more confidence I attempted to connect us. I wasn't sure how to go about it, so I used the one thing I knew how to. My imagination. In my mind I created a beam of light, shooting from my body to Alahn's. Not knowing what he looked like, I imagined him as a shadow. Realizing I had been closing my eyes during my attempt to connect us, I snapped them open. And there stood a man, covered in small purple scales. He had neither a mouth nor toes, and his ears were small holes on the sides of his head.

"Well done." He said. *"I had all the time in the world to figure this out in my cell, but you... you figured it out in a matter of minutes. You're a smart one, aren't you?"*

"Yes, I am." I Replied. *"And now you're going to explain what's going on."*

"Right." Alahn said, putting his hands in a warning motion. *"This'll be a lot to take in."*

"After the last few days I've had? Try me."

"Very well. You obviously do not know of your cosmic blood, or of the powers you wield. I will try my best to instruct you."

"But what do you mean I have cosmic blood? What are you talking about?"

"The cosmics are a race, just like humans, living out in the cosmos. I have unnaturally joined their race, but you... your bloodline is connected to them."

I had absolutely no idea what any of this meant. My family heritage was not in any way intertwined into some alien species, that I knew of. The farthest name back the Salt family could track was Cast.

"So, you're saying," I began. *"That I'm part human and part alien?"*

"In simple terms, yes." Came the reply. *"Now if we're going to stand a chance, you're going to need to learn how to hone in your new powers. Use the same method you did to bridge yourself to me. That seemed to work for you. Focus and channel your cosmic energy into your hands. See what you can do."*

And I did. I imagined my body was a circuit, and my hands were the output, expelling some unknown power. My hands began to glow a bright purple, and waves of purple air were flowing from them.

"That is the purple aura." Alahn said. *"One of many, but specifically the one cosmics can tap into. It provides mystical powers, can be used as a weapon, a shield, and for the most experienced... something physics cannot yet explain, to the untrained simpleton seeming like magic. The*

purple aura has even seemed to connect me to knowledge former users have passed down." I looked up at him.

"Have I had this my whole life?" I asked.

"As far as I can tell. Go on. Test it out."

He said it could be used as weapon, a shield, and... something modern science had not caught up to yet. I began seeing what I could do in that order. I thought of a blast coming from my hand, and one did. A thick purple beam shot from my right hand and disappeared into the dark void.

"Very good." Said Alahn, mock applauding.

I then moved on to the shield. I pictured a rounded wall coming from my extended hands covering the front of my body. And so did one appear.

"It's incredible," Alahn said, studying my shield. *"How new this is to you and yet how well you wield it. You could be the one to stop him."*

"Him?" I said, discontinuing my shield. *"Do you mean the one who's been causing all the violence in this town? Who is he? Where is he?"*

Alahn advanced towards me.

"I think you'll be able to process this safely," he said. He placed his hands on either side of my head and touched his forehead against mine. *"This should explain enough for you to find him."*

His body glowed, and suddenly my mind was filled with images, and memories of Alahn's. Events relating to this town flooded into my head, flashing at speeds unimaginable.

"Use these." I heard above the chaos. *"Find me. Come alone."*

My head felt like it was going to explode. The images wouldn't stop, everything that had happened to Alahn in this town was suddenly happening to me.

"P- Please no more!" I thought as loud as I could. *"Make it stop! It's too much! I—"*

Everything swirled around, and the intense darkness was replaced by an unimaginably bright flash. And then I could think no more.

***   ***

Alahn was back in his containment cell, disconnected from the mind void. The conversation with Lloyd had gone much better this time, and now that he had transferred the information into his mind, all he could do was wait. He spotted Ezekiel walking by through the thick glass that separated him from the outside world.

***"Off to visit your golden boy?"* Alahn thought to him.**

"It is time." Was Ezekiel's answer. "Its mind has finally come to. And you know what that means."

Alahn watched as Ezekiel descended the staircase leading to his creation. Alahn did know what it meant. It meant Ezekiel's plan was finally about to come to fruition. He would use his created cosmic to destroy the human world, before the next day was done. Or not. He was not finished mutating into a cosmic, and neither was his team. That meant there was still time for Lloyd to stop him. Or at least, Alahn hoped so.

"Hello." Ezekiel said, opening the door between him, and his cosmic. It was hovering right in front of the door, peering out its small window.

"Do you know who I am?"

It locked its eyes with Ezekiel's.

"Yes." It put into Ezekiel's thoughts. *"You're father."*

"That's right." Ezekiel said. "Do you know what you're here for?"

"Yes." It said once again. *"To serve father."*

"And what does father want?"

"Father wants what I want."

"Tell me."

"The destruction of all humans."

Ezekiel smiled. He rolled up his sleeve to show his new son the scales that were etching themselves along his wrist.

"Father was once like you," he said. "And father will be like you once again.

"But I need to become faster. Can you do that?"

"Anything, for father."

It placed its hand on the patch of scales on his wrist. It glowed bright purple, and the scales spread all across Ezekiel, until he was a human-cosmic hybrid like Alahn.

"Father is pleased." Ezekiel said. "Oh, how I've missed this. I can feel the power flowing through my veins like it once did!"

Ezekiel used his newfound cosmic abilities to reform his appearance to that of the days long ago. He had a human frame, but purple skin and cosmic capabilities. He looked like the days of when he was Oliver Cast. But of course, Oliver Cast was long gone now. It was Ezekiel who would rule this new world.

"Come," Ezekiel said, walking from the large water hole. "It's time you met the rest of the family."

The cosmic left its former home and followed its "father". They passed Alahn, who looked shocked to see Ezekiel fully mutated. Ezekiel brought his cosmic into a room which held Veronica and the rest of his team.

"Master," one said, looking at the ground. "Is it time for our glorious transformation from human, to something better?"

"No." Ezekiel said. "You were always human. You will always be poison." He looked at the cosmic.

"Kill them."

The cosmic held out its claws and shot small blasts of energy at each of their chests. The shocked look on their faces were the last thing they had before falling to the ground, dead. All the men were killed. The cosmic looked to Veronica.

"Spare her." Ezekiel said. "You shall make her like you have made me."

"Y-you said you would let them reign with you." Veronica said, clearly stunned.

"I could never do that." Ezekiel said, walking close to Veronica.

"You're the only human I love."

He tilted her head slightly up and kissed her. Ezekiel needed a bride in the new world he was creating, to repopulate the earth with cosmics as he planned. He had courted this one called Veronica for that purpose and converted her to his cause. Whether his feelings for her were love, or simply using her for his grand design was beside the point to Ezekiel.

"Now come," Ezekiel said, pulling away. "Become like me. You and I shall rule together, restart the world." He gestured towards the cosmic.

"Alongside the one I shall call, Genesis."

CHAP**8**TER

Quanton entered the room where Cyrus sat with a couple other big names that ran this organization.

"Quanton," Cyrus said. "I'm pleased you could join us on such short notice.

Please, have a seat."

Quanton sat down in the empty chair beside the round meeting table.

"What's going on?" he asked.

"The situation at the Coated Coast has escalated," Cyrus explained. "If you recall Karina was ordered to contact us every night, and brief us on the day that had passed, and only not to if she was in grave danger, and scenario in which she couldn't." Quanton nodded.

"She did not contact us last night, or this morning."

Quanton leaned back in his chair.

"That can't be good." He stated. "What're we going to do about it?"

Cyrus gestured to the three other men sitting at the table. They were each leaders, like Cyrus, of a school run by this organization.

"I have brought these three here to discuss that." Cyrus said. "We have come to a consensus, that we shall each spare some of our elite combatants to take siege of the town, and hopefully find out what has become of Karina, and stop Ezekiel."

"Okay." Quanton agreed. "And I assume I am here to pair with Lloyd?"

"Yes." Cyrus answered. "We're just hoping he's alright. Your job, Quanton, is now to protect him, heaven willing he's still alive. If Lloyd gets killed, all this will be futile."

"And you've told these guys your little legend?"

"They know, yes."

"When do we head out?" Quanton asked.

"Now." The man to the left of Cyrus said. "This whole situation has blown up, and frankly I don't know why we're standing around here talking."

"Right." Cyrus said, standing up. "My troops are armed, and in the copter. Gather yours, and we'll meet up at the town."

Quanton followed Cyrus out to his helicopter.

Here we go, he thought. *Now it begins.*

***   ***

I woke with a massive headache. Groaning as I sat up, I checked my surroundings. It looked as though I was on Ms. Ross's sofa in her living room. Standing up, I ran my fingers through my hair. My last conversation with Alahn had ended awfully. What did he mean "use these"? What had he given me? The closest thing I could figure, was Alahn had somehow given me his memories. But I didn't seem to recall anything that had happened to me.

Hearing the voices of conversation from the kitchen, I headed over to find Zahna and Earl sitting at the table having a breakfast of toast. This reminded me of how hungry I was.

"You're finally up." Earl said. "Dude, you were out for a while that time."

"Yeah," I said, taking the liberty to get myself some bread from a bread box on the counter. "It got... pretty crazy in there."

"So, what happened?" Zahna asked. "Did you talk to Earl's father?" I popped the bread in the old-fashioned toaster.

"Yes." I said.

"What'd he say?" Earl asked, interested in anything to do with his father.

I glanced around the house.

"Is Ms. Ross around?" I wondered, ignoring Earl for the moment. "I don't want her knowing much about this."

"She woke up when we arrived at around one a.m." Zahna explained. "She's sleeping in now."

"What'd you guys tell her?"

My toast popped, and I placed it on a paper napkin, while I looked for condiments.

"Same thing." Zahna said. "I told her that Earl was a friend of ours who had got mixed up in her husband's killers' business as well... and that you were knocked out from falling downstairs. She wanted to call the police but seeing as none of us are really on their good side we convinced her not to."

I normally prefer chunky peanut butter but seeing her inventory it appeared that today I would have to settle for smooth. I sat down at the table, purposely next to Zahna.

"Good." I said, before taking a bite. "What was your question again, Earl?"

"I was wondering what my dad told you."

"Right. He told me I had some kind of bloodline, that connected me to the cosmics." I said, finally answering Earl's question. I didn't give them the full scope of it, as I was still processing it myself. "He said I had some kind of power."

"The cosmics?" Earl said, puzzled. "Who the heck are they?" Suddenly my mind was flooded with the answer. "I think," I started. "I think we saw one in the aquarium." "They're called cosmics?" Zahna asked.

"Yes." My mind was unlocking more and more info about them. "They're an ancient race that once lived with the humans... but they left for some reason. Ezekiel is trying to-" I paused.

"Ezekiel." I said again. "That's who we're up against. Ezekiel is his name."

"But how do you know all this?" Earl said. "Did my dad tell you all that in that short amount of time?" I shook my head.

"No, not verbally anyway. He transferred what he knew into my mind somehow," I looked at Earl. "Earl, your dad has become a cosmic."

"My dad has become a cosmic?!" Earl exclaimed. "What- how?"

"Ezekiel did experiments on him... to see if it would work, so he could do it on himself...."

My blood ran cold as a new memory entered my mind.

"Oh, gosh." I said. "Ezekiel wants to wipe out the human race and bring rise to an age of cosmics. He himself will now be a cosmic and take charge."

"How could he do that?" Zahna said. "Wipe out the entire human race?"

"Find me. Come alone." The thought seemingly came to my head out of nowhere, like a distant whisper.

"I—" I started. "I don't know. But I do know where they are." "My father told you, didn't he?" Earl inquired.

"Yes." I said. "He told me to come alone." "Like the heck that's happening." Zahna said.

"My thoughts exactly." I replied.

Unlocking more and more information as we went, I explained exactly where Ezekiel's hide out was, and some of the schematics of the place.

As we planned our attack, Earl would also ask questions about his father. I explained as best I could, but Alahn didn't know everything behind Ezekiel's plan, so some I could not answer. When we were satisfied with our strike plan, we discussed what would be our priorities.

"Freeing Alahn is top on our list," I told them. "As he seems to have some powers that could be useful while combating Ezekiel. Next would be, of course, stopping Ezekiel. Springing Karina we'll have to do somewhere in there too. And to make things clear, I don't want any of you to get hurt. If I tell you I got something, or you need to escape, you better listen to me."

And our planning went on, with minor disagreements here and there, explanation demands a couple of times, but in the end, we had an efficient, if not totally awesome plan of action. We told Ms. Ross we would be out for a bit, not wanting to worry her with the truth. As I led my team to our destination point, I noticed how nervous each of them looked, and how scared I actually felt. The *world* depended on us, not just this town anymore. And we were just kids.

"You each know what to do, right?" I reconfirmed.

They nodded. We had been silent for a while, the gravity of the situation still sinking in on us. But I couldn't stop thinking: *Did my agency know about this?*

Did they think it was just a minor crime spree? But if they did know, why?

Our destination approached closer, and closer, until we were there, finally ready to confront the man behind all this.

***   ***

The helicopters landed just south of the town, the troops heading the rest of the way on foot. They were following a ping from Karina, via a small tracker they implanted into her skin in case a situation like this should arise. Cyrus and the other commanders led squadrons in all directions around the ping to surround their opponent. Eventually they came to the Coated Coast train station.

"You seeing this?" Cyrus heard from his earpiece com. "It's a public place. How could they be based here?"

"Let's find out." Cyrus said. "On my call, everyone storm the place. On three… two… one… NOW!"

The mini army burst through the doors, from the front and back, and found themselves in the crummy train station. A thick middle-aged woman was looking shocked behind a large wooden desk.

"Heavens!" she cried, in a crackly voice. "Now, what is this all about?"

"You're going to have to clear the premises ma'am." one of Cyrus's peers said. "By order of the C.I.A."

"Dear me," she said, ruffling through some papers and utensils on her desk.

"Let me just…"

"You need to exit, NOW."

"Hold on, I just have to…"

Suddenly a soldier leapt from his formation and tackled the woman to the ground.

"What the Sam Hill are you crazies doing now?!" she roared. "I have my rights."

"Look." The soldier said, handcuffing the woman and walking towards the desk. He picked up a small rectangular device with a couple of buttons on it.

"She was going to press this."

"It must be an alarm system," one of them said. "She's working with them." 'What do you know about this?" Cyrus asked.

"I don't know what you're talking about." The woman responded defiantly.

"Miss, you're going to be spending a long time behind bars as it is," Cyrus commented. "Do you really want to make this harder?" She looked like she was contemplating this.

"Will I get any amnesty if I talk?" She said finally.

"We'll see." One of the commanders said.

"Under the desk." The woman said, pointing. "You'll find a passageway."

A soldier bent under the desk and peeled away some fake tiles. Under was a downwards tunnel, with rungs leading all the way down.

"I'll go first," Cyrus said. "Quanton, you go last."

The professor nodded. As soon as another would fit, they climbed on down. At the bottom they found a door, which they slowly opened, and as soon as the coast was claimed clear, filed in. They were now inside a large room, with what looked like a broken round aquarium tank, and stairs leading to a metal platform.

"Keep your positions," Cyrus said quietly. "We don't know where they are."

Spreading out in the room, the squadrons and their commanders each took up a strategic position, should anyone come in.

After waiting a while, Cyrus heard on his com:

"My team and I are going through that door over there. We've been waiting here too long."

Cyrus saw one of the commanders followed by five troops barge through the door that led to an adjoining room.

"We'll take the door on that platform." Cyrus heard through his com again.

Now only he and another commander's squadron remained in the room to spring an ambush. Cyrus shifted his gun in his hand and tried to crouch down lower behind the staircase. Hiding was never a comfortable sport. A minute later he heard from his com again.

"Guys, we've found something." It said. "It- it's like some sort of mythical beast. It talks through our thoughts from a containment room it's inside, and… it claims its Alahn Alten the man who went missing a few weeks ago!"

"Don't trust it," someone answered. "And definitely don't let it out."

"Hold on," Cyrus heard again. "Someone's coming." Cyrus heard shuffling feet and moving bodies.

"Do you need back up?" Cyrus asked.

"Negative. It's just a man and a woman. FREEZE WHERE YOU ARE!"

They must have seen them.

"My, my." A male voice said in the background. "Look Veronica, someone sent us a gift and didn't bother to wrap it."

"Get your hands in the air!"

"So pushy. Genesis, would you do the honors?"

Suddenly Cyrus heard men shouting, and guns firing.

"What in the—" the commander was saying. "Back up! Yes, we do need back up, AHHIIIEEEE!"

Cyrus's com went silent.

"GO, GO!" Cyrus shouted to his squadron and burst through the door. They ran down a hallway and passed the creature the other commander had mentioned.

"You have to let me out!" Came into Cyrus's mind. *"You can't do anything to them! It's a suicide mission without another cosmic on your side!"*

Cyrus took no heed of its warnings. Continuing to run with his crew of five, he came to a halt. There standing in the hallway was a purple man, and a purple woman, preceded by a scaly creature Cyrus made out as a cosmic.

"Why even try?" the man said. Cyrus decided he must be Ezekiel. "By the end of the day, you pathetic bags of flesh won't even exist anymore."

Genesis barred his claws and stared intently at Cyrus and his crew. The second commander from the main room arrived behind him.

"My thoughts exactly, Genesis." Ezekiel said. "Do it."

Genesis leapt forward; claws extended at Cyrus. He rolled out of the way at the last second, just for one of his soldiers to get torn into. Guns fired at the cosmic, but to no avail. Its dark, purple scales were near impenetrable. Cyrus wanted to help his men, but he knew Ezekiel was the real danger here. Gripping his gun, he charged towards Ezekiel. Barrel blazing, Cyrus was stunned to see Ezekiel flick his hands and all the shells go to the side. With a wave of his hand, Ezekiel also threw Cyrus into the wall beside him. Not giving him a moment to catch his breath, Ezekiel picked Cyrus up by the shoulders and slammed him against the wall.

"How did you know about me," he barked into Cyrus's face. "How'd you know I was here?!"

"We found your archives,' Cyrus said, grunting through pain. "What, you think they would remain hidden forever? Been around a while, haven't you *Oliver Cast*."

"And if you have read them," Ezekiel said, thudding Cyrus's head on the ground. "You should know that Oliver Cast failed and is no more. It is I, Ezekiel who will rule over the earth of the cosmics."

Ezekiel was about to deliver the finishing blow when suddenly he was tackled to the ground by a soldier.

"Run commander!" he shouted.

Cyrus listened to the advice and dashed the other way. He tried not to listen to the screams of his comrade. Cyrus viewed the scene around him. The team who had searched the door of the platform had found their way back, unfortunately without Karina. But even with the fresh troops the battle was being lost. The enemy was largely outnumbered, yet they tore into Cyrus's and the other commander's crew like they were paper. With Genesis, Ezekiel, and Veronica all possessing cosmic powers they weren't going to win this battle any time soon. Cyrus decided there was only one thing to do that could possibly help. Running back the way he came, he returned to the containment room that held Alahn.

"You'll never win!" Was forced into Cyrus's brain. "You need me! Let me out!"

"I'm working on it." Cyrus thought back, starting on the many locks on the door. "Hold on just a minute."

Cyrus worked as fast as he could, trying to unclip, unlatch, or pull locks away before Ezekiel figured out what he was doing. Finally, they were all off, and before Cyrus could open it, the door was flung off its hinges. Without even a thanks Alahn flew off to the battle sight. Cyrus running close behind him, witnessed Alahn diving into Genesis, and then throw a purple blast at Ezekiel and Veronica. The element of surprise throwing their enemies off, the squadrons and their commanders were able to retreat. Their numbers had been greatly decreased, and where they had started with twenty men, they now had only seven. Reaching the large room with the platform the crew took a moment to catch their breath.

"What on earth do we do now?" a soldier asked. "Those guys are like a force of nature!"

"There's been too many casualties," Cyrus said, "All we can do now is retreat."

"What about Lloyd," the last remaining commander besides Cyrus asked.

"You were the one who was so adamant he was the only way to stop this."

"He's right here," said Quanton, turning around. Next to his side was Lloyd, and two other children. "And he's got some quite interesting news."

CHAP**9**TER

It was full on cosmic versus cosmic. Alahn would use his new-found abilities and powers, just to have them countered by Genesis. It didn't help that he was outnumbered three to one either. Ezekiel and Veronica would often pitch in on beating him up as well. Firing a burst of aura towards Genesis, the genetically engineered cosmic caught it between his claws and shot back at Alahn. Leaping out of the way and watching the orb crash into the wall, Alahn was hit by a different aura ball fired by Ezekiel. This blasted Alahn a good ten feet and sent him sprawling on the ground.

"You don't want to do this!" He thought desperately to Genesis. *"Humans and cosmics can live together again! Ezekiel is wrong!"*

"How dare you say such a thing!" An angry voice shot into Alahn's head. He realized when he broadcasted his thoughts to communicate, they must have also reached Ezekiel. *"You yourself told me there were no more cosmics beyond earth! Because of you flesh bags the cosmics no longer had refuge and were hunted and consumed by the Others!"*

The conversation had given Alahn time to stand up.

"Who are these Others you keep speaking of," Alahn asked Ezekiel, aware of the aura ball Genesis held in its hand. *"And who are they to defeat the "mighty" cosmics?"*

"They were the death of us," Ezekiel thought. *"Time, and time again, until this planet provided us rest. But by gosh, they won't be again."*

Genesis launched its aura ball, probably by a thought command Ezekiel had given it, so fast Alahn barely had time to duck. Giving up on the ranged battle tactic, Alahn dived at Genesis, claws extended. Slashing at its chest, bashing its head, Alahn would have all but obliterated a human, but only inflicted wounds upon Genesis. Genesis leapt backwards. Scales were ripped open around its body, and purple blood escaped from them.

"Father help!" Genesis weakly thought to Ezekiel, but before the thought was sent Ezekiel was already charging at Alahn.

Ezekiel grasped Alahn's throat in a choke hold and concentrated all his cosmic power into that hand. As a result, it glowed brilliantly. Alahn grabbed at his hand, and tried to pull it off, but it was much too strong. Ezekiel's grip was unimaginably tight, as all of his power was gathered there.

"Stop," Alahn thought. *"Ezekiel please stop…"*

"Aww, poor Alahn." Ezekiel replied. *"All alone, and about to die. And just so you know,"* Ezekiel thought this part menacingly. *"Your son's next."*

"No…"

Alahn couldn't breathe. Not even a scrap of air. The light began to fade from his eyes… then Alahn fell limp. Ezekiel tossed him to the side.

"Come my love," he said to Veronica. "And come my prodigy," he said to Genesis. "We have a world to make reborn."

***   ***

My new memories guided the three of us to the train station where I had first arrived in Coated Coast. Upon entering we saw a soldier whose uniform I recognized as a part of my organization. He was guarding the woman I had met here a couple days ago. Beneath the large wooden desk, they were standing by, was a hole with metal prongs leading down to a compound which I just suddenly remembered. I don't think I'll ever get used to borrowing someone's recollections. The guard seemed to recognize me.

"You," he said in a deep voice. "We thought you had been apprehended."

"Well I have not been." I said. "What are you guys doing here?"

"Well," the soldier replied. "Surely you must have realized that this is no ordinary term by now."

"Yeah. Either that or you guys are insane."

From the corner of my eye I could see the confused looks Zahna and Earl were giving me.

"We should not discuss things here." The soldier replied. He beckoned to the woman he had cuffed and gagged, and my two comrades. "Not with this woman and those two kids."

"You're right." I replied. I pointed to the hole in the floor. "I'm going down there."

I started to advance, but he grabbed my shoulder.

"No." he commanded. "We were all instructed to keep you safe."

"Aww." I said. "Now I feel special. Listen," I began in a more serious tone. "I don't fully understand what's going on here, but I do know I'm involved, and I can't turn my back on this town now. And this place... Coated Coast... it's not the only area in danger. Ezekiel, he's a nihilist. He's got a much bigger picture in mind. I can't just stand by and watch his plans unfold." The guard stared intently at me.

"How?" He said finally. "How do you know so much?"

"Honestly," I said. "I'm not entirely sure. But if you're not going to let us by, we'll invite ourselves in." I looked at Zahna.

"Hit it." I said.

She threw one of her harmless gas bombs just to confuse him while we slipped down the hole. Fortunately for us it worked. Before the smoke cleared, we had touched our feet to the ground at the end tunnel. I found myself face to face with a thick metal door. Turning behind me, I looked at Zahna and Earl. Before I could say anything, Zahna spoke up.

"What was that up there, Lloyd?" She asked, an accusatory tone in her voice. "You talked like you knew that guy or knew of him. What's going on?"

I was in between a rock and hard place now. Part of the initiation into my agency was swearing your allegiance to it as secrecy, not even letting people closest to you know about it, if they weren't involved.

"Know him?" I said. "Of course not. I guess I kind of work with him." Zahna still didn't look impressed.

"I asked you if you were a detective before, Lloyd." She said. "But this time I'm plainly asking; who are you?"

"I'm Lloyd Salt." I replied. "And that's all you need to know."

It's never fun disappointing a pretty girl, but when they give you that *look*, the look of annoyance, almost like they're mad at you, that's just the worst. During our discussion Earl just stood there, observing.

"I don't expect you guys to come with me." I started, finally able to say my piece. "This is my fight, and I would never want to put you in deliberate danger. I'll perfectly understand if you climb back up that ladder." None of them responded right away. Finally, Earl spoke up.

"My dad was the reason for all the good things in life." He said. "Striving for good grades, always trying to be the best on sports teams, learning his trade... all to get his approval. And now it's my time to really prove myself." He stood a little taller. And I felt a bit more confident.

"I'm not giving up on him now."

"Good man." I said, patting his shoulder.

153

I looked at Zahna.

"I'm through running from these guys." She simply said. "Time to teach these jackboots a lesson."

I couldn't stifle my grin. I didn't know if I considered these two friends just yet, but they were there for me. They were my team.

"Thank you." I said. "It means a lot."

I thought back to when I was in that mind void. I concentrated my mind on creating a cosmic circuit around me, extended my arms and recreated the shield around my body. Zahna and Earl gasped.

"Stay behind me." I said, advancing closer to the door. "We don't know what we'll be facing in there."

"Lloyd!" Earl stutters. "You- but, what?!"

"I don't entirely know myself." I replied. "Apparently I'm linked to the cosmic race. These are the quirks that come with it." I looked back at them.

"Brace yourselves."

And with that I threw open the door. I intensified my shield and gritted my teeth. I heard gun shots, but they weren't directed towards us. In fact, no hostiles were in the room. We walked in, and I glanced around. The place seemed familiar to me, a side effect of Alahn's and my memory transfer. I closed my shield down.

"Well that was anti-climactic." I said. "But don't slack yet. Those gun shots are getting closer."

Zahna seemed like she was going to say something but was interrupted.

"Lloyd," a voice said. A man stepped out from behind the remnants of an aquarium tank. I recognized him immediately.

"Professor Quanton." I replied.

"Lloyd, we need to get you out of here," he continued, running up to us and ushering me out. "Our entire task force is dying up there, we don't stand a chance."

"You guys knew this was happening." I said, staring defiantly at him. "You knew it was happening and you sent a kid?! What is wrong with you!"

Quanton looked anxiously over his shoulder, as if he was expecting an armada to burst through the door behind him any second.

"Well," he said. "You're not just a kid."

I fired up my cosmic shield.

"No kidding." I said. "Now you need to finally tell me what's going on." Before he could, multiple footsteps ran into the room.

"What on earth do we do now!" a panicked voice said. "Those guys are like a force of nature!"

"There's been too many casualties," said another.

"All we can do now is wait."

"What about Lloyd?" I perked up at this comment. Looking at the beat up few I recognized one of them as Cyrus, the leader of the branch of the C.I.A. I belonged to. "You were the one who was so adamant that he was the only way to stop this."

Quanton turned around.

"He's right here." He said. "And he's got some interesting news."

Cyrus looked at us, and his eyes widened when he saw the cosmic shield I was forming around myself.

"So, you've figured it out." He said. "And not a moment too soon."

"No thanks to you." I was quite irritated with my organization at this point.

"You have some explaining to do, Cyrus."

"Um, guys?" Earl said, a bit timidly. "Those footsteps are getting close."

He was right. In fact, they were right on top of us. The door flew off its hinges as a creature, much like the one I saw in the mind void, led two purple humans behind it. There was a man and a woman, the girl I recognized from the aquarium. The man must have been Ezekiel.

"Get Lloyd out of here," Cyrus shouted. "Go!"

A pair of rough hands grabbed onto my shoulder and began dragging me to the door.

"Nope," I said, struggling to get released from the soldier that was holding me.

"I came here to rescue someone and stop Ezekiel. I'm not leaving until I have."

Using my newfound abilities, I made my hands glow bright purple, and using a reinforcement of "purple aura," knocked the soldier off of me. He grunted and tumbled to the ground. Regretting doing that to someone on my side, I am back into the center of the room where everyone else was leaving.

"Lloyd!" I heard Quanton's voice.

I ignored him. I finally had the chance to face the man who was behind all the murders I had seen in this town, behind Karina's kidnapping, and I wasn't about to run away. This man had caused too much trouble for this town. Despite my angry emotions towards Ezekiel, once I was in front of him and staring him down, I felt like it was foolish idea to not go with the rest of the crew. Ezekiel glared down menacingly at me. I tried to keep my knees from buckling with fear.

"We've got a brave specimen here today." Ezekiel said, his purple face glaring down at me. "Brave, or should I say, stupid."

He put his arm on my shoulder, and my entire body tingled with fear. He was right. This was stupid. I was blinded because of the anger I felt towards him and went in without a plan. I heard shouting and guns cocking behind me, but the cosmic to the right shoulder of Ezekiel waved its hand, and the shouts were replaced by thuds.

"I know who you are." Ezekiel said. "You're the boy who's interfered with us, time and time again. At the mansion, in the aquarium. And I see you've teamed up with the girl who has plagued us as well. "

He gestured towards Zahna and Earl who had lingered behind as well.

157

"And the boy who we've needed up to now. Earl was it? Yes. He would've been quite the bargaining chip with his father, even more so if we had him in person."

"My father." Earl said. I could hear the fear in his voice. "Where is he?"

Ezekiel averted his attention from me and looked at Earl.

"Your father was a smart man." He said. "But not smart enough to know how to save his own skin."

Earl's color was draining from his face.

"What're you saying?" He managed.

"There was a bit of a rebellion your father put up." Ezekiel said, almost smiling.

I felt awful. I knew what was coming next. Just like I had failed to save Anderson, or the maids, or even Karina, I had failed to save Earl's father, Alahn.

"You could say," Ezekiel continued. "That he was killed in self-defense."

I took a glance at Earl. He looked like everything bad in the world had been thrown onto him then and there. But his look of unimaginable loss was soon replaced by one of seething anger.

"Earl," I heard Zahna whispering. "I'm so sorry..."

"YOU!" Earl suddenly shouted pointing at Ezekiel. He had anger and courage in his voice like I had never heard him speak before.

Apparently, that was the end of his sentence though, as he charged towards Ezekiel and me.

"Earl, don't!" I yelled towards him, but it was too late.

"Genesis," Ezekiel said, probably the name of the cosmic beside him.

Genesis leapt forward at Earl—claws extended. And from that point on everything seemed to happen in slow motion. You hear about certain events in peoples' lives seemingly happening in slow-mo, you read about it in books, but you don't really believe it until you experience it. Zahna was on the heels of Earl, probably attempting to stop him. Earl was running at full speed towards Ezekiel. Genesis was about to shred Earl apart. I was in the grasp of the most dangerous man I had met. Of course, I didn't have time to think. I consider it more of an instinct what I did in that moment. Charging my hands to send an aura blast like I had in the mind void, I pressed one hand against Ezekiel's chest about to fire and turned to fire off a blast from my left hand at Genesis. A blast most comparable to a boomerang, shot from my hand and barreled into Genesis sending him off course and somewhere across the room. I didn't see what had become of Ezekiel until I turned and saw him sliding down a wall and crash to the floor. The woman who had been to the left of Ezekiel clearly did not have panic training, and just stood there looking shocked. I had successfully fixed that problem, but like Professor Quanton would always say about time travel, the solution to one problem often springs the origin for another. The variable of the charging Earl was still on the table, and with nothing in his way, and no time to stop himself, we collided and found ourselves sprawled on top of one another on the floor. I had gained the element of surprise, and a really good position, just to soon be lying on my face, a terrible position. Thankfully Zahna thought fast on her feet as well and threw down one of her famous smoke bombs adding another element of surprise, and I soon found myself being hoisted up by adult hands and quickly guided into another room. I heard a door slam shut and my vision cleared. The adult hands I had felt turned out to be Professor Quanton's, as he stood there between Zahna and Earl. We were in a wide hallway, farther from where Cyrus had told me to go.

"Everyone good?" Quanton asked, looking us over.

"Good?!" Earl snapped, with surprising velocity. "I just learned that my father is dead! I am nowhere near "good"!"

I felt sympathy for Earl, but this was no time to grieve.

"Guys, we gotta move." I said. "Come on."

We ran down the wide hallway passing a large room with a glass viewing area to look inside. The glass had scratch gouges through the center. As we continued on, we came across a body that resembled a cosmic like Genesis.

"Earl," I said. "That's him. That's Alahn."

"Dad," Earl said, his voice cracking. He bent down over him. "I'm sorry I didn't make it too you in time."

"Maybe just in time, son." A weak voice said, my brain picking it up as well as Earl's.

"Dad!" Earl perked up. "You're alive! But how…?"

"I realized I couldn't beat all three of them." Alahn continued, as Earl helped prop him against the wall. Zahna was looking very amazed at the telepathic speaking, Quanton looking like he was thinking of any scientific way this could be possible. Earl was so relieved he didn't even think of the oddity of it. *"Let Ezekiel think he finished me off… but I'm almost done for anyhow."*

"There must be some way to help you." Earl said. We heard banging on the door we had locked behind us. "But quickly, or we're all going to be toast."

"I share properties of the cosmics now." Alahn said. *"I can heal in cosmic waters. Ezekiel possesses some up ahead, but I can barely walk. I shall slow you down to much…"*

"No," I said. Alahn looked up at me. "not another person will die on my term. Whether it's my fault," I stared at Quanton, "or not. Quanton, Earl, you help get Alahn to the cosmic waters. Zahna you lead the way. I'll take up the rear in case they catch up."

Everyone began taking their positions. Soon, along with the injured Alahn, we began hobbling our way to the cosmic waters Alahn spoke of. But as I predicted Ezekiel and company were catching up. Charging my hands for an aura blast, I slowly continued to walk backwards.

"Go as fast as you can." I told my crew. "And don't come back for me should things go south."

And with that I charged forward, and at the first sight of a body, fired off discs of aura from my hands. They must have connected with somebody, as shouting and crashing ensued. Advancing forward slightly, I saw Veronica collecting herself. But only Veronica. Where were Ezekiel and...? My thoughts were interrupted by Veronica suddenly firing aura blasts of her own. Making a shield faster than I thought possible, the aura discs collided with that rather than me, creating a bass like *BOOM!* and inching me backwards a pace.

"You," Veronica said. "You're the boy who eluded me at the aquarium. You won't be so lucky this time."

"I'd say its lucky for you that you didn't have to face me." I retorted. "What'd you do with the creature in that tank anyhow?"

"Disposed of it." Veronica said, as I became aware that she was inching closer. "Didn't have a need for it. Just like we don't have a need for you."

She lunged forwards at me, but I was prepared. Somersaulting forward, all Veronica grasped was empty air. She stuck the landing though and doubled back shooting an aura blast. Not having time to dodge it, I considered myself lucky that it just grazed my shoulder. It still hurt like heck though and flipped me in the air. I fell on the cold metal floor, a headache exploding within my skull.

"I see you don't have any of your girlfriends helping you this time." Veronica taunted on. "Or any friends for that matter. They ditch you to your fate or something?"

The entire arm where the blast hit was burning, I just barely stood up. "Yeah well," I began. "Your mad boyfriend doesn't seem to be present. Where'd he get off to?" Veronica just smiled.

"You'd like to know wouldn't you." Was her only response.

And then it finally occurred to me. Like the baby cosmic in the aquarium she was a diversion. Ezekiel and Genesis were off fulfilling his apocalyptic dream while she and I fought in here. I kicked myself for not thinking of it sooner. If they were leaving the compound anyway, what need would they have for sending all their forces after us? This was not the fight I needed to be fighting. I had to find some way to get rid of her and get out of here. As I remembered something I had seen a little ways back, the way to do that occurred to me.

It's amazing how fast your brain can think under stress because as I was realizing all this a total of about three seconds had probably elapsed, and I still had time to dodge the aura blast Veronica was sending my way. It crashed harmlessly into the wall, creating a singed look against it.

"I'll take my leave now." I said and began running back towards the containment cell I had seen.

She was close behind me, occasionally firing aura blasts which I had to counter with my trademark shield. Our deadly chase didn't last very long as our destination was close. When we arrived at the containment cell site, I allowed myself to be hit by an aura blast. Purposely falling next to the door to the cell, I took note about how bad a full-on aura blast hurt. It felt as though every nerve in my body was on fire. At least as I struggled to stand, I didn't have to act to sell the realness.

"I got you cornered boy." Veronica said. "Your abilities are impressive. If you weren't so bent on constantly getting in our way Ezekiel may even offer you a position in his new world."

I silently prayed that she wouldn't notice the hand I was using to pop myself against the wall, was in fact opening the door into the containment cell.

"It's a shame such talent must go to waste." Veronica continued, placing a glowing hand on my chest. "Any last sentiments?"

"Yeah." I said. "Gotcha."

I threw open the door while at the same time seizing Veronica by the shoulder with my aura enhanced arm, and throwing her in. I slammed the door shut and latched all the locks shut. I heard Veronica shouting and cursing at me, and bangs and blasts of her attempting to escape. Clearly the cell was made to contain one with cosmic abilities, and all her efforts were in vain. My body was telling me to stop and rest, but there was no time. Ezekiel was somehow going to erase humanity from existence, and whether that was possible or not it was now my job to stop him. Grabbing my still throbbing shoulder, I ran to the exit where I would soon confront Ezekiel.

***   ***

Quanton and Earl trudged on, Alahn draped over their shoulders. They heard commotion from Lloyd's battle behind them, but they

heeded his command not to come back for him. On their trek they came across another cell. Banging was coming from the iron door. Zahna paused.

"Another prisoner." She said. "Should we let whoever it is out?"

"Hold on". Alahn said. "I'll ask him who he is."

To Zahna and the rest there was silence for a moment.

"My name's Karina!" Came a muffled female voice from inside. "Please, get me out of here!"

"Karina!" Zahna exclaimed. "That's Lloyd's partner."

She hurriedly unlocked and unlatched the door and opened it up. Karina wearily came out.

"Thanks guys." She said. "Man I'm hungry. Um... where's Lloyd?"

"Holding off Ezekiel and company." Zahna replied. "We need to heal Alahn there, and we don't have much time. You probably don't have much energy but try to keep up."

Karina smiled despite herself. This girl was starting to sound like Lloyd. They hustled off, and Karina did her best to stay with them. They had to descend a small staircase but soon after the bottom they arrived at where Alahn said the cosmic water deposit was.

"Behind that door." Alahn said, beckoning towards a thick metal door with a small window in it.

Zahna went over and, as always, had to unlock and pry open the door. Inside was a vat of what looked like normal looking water.

"Just put me in," said Alahn, "I can do the rest."

Quanton and Earl helped him to the edge of the water vat.

"Good luck dad." Said Earl.

And with that they heaved him in. Alahn sunk and disappeared into the dark waters. For a moment nothing happened. Earl held his breath in anticipation. Then suddenly the waters began to glow, much like the night before, but a more purple hue than the bright blue they had previously seen. This was a healing glow, not a feeding glow, borrowing power from the purple aura itself. Soon the glowing subsided, and Alahn's body was seen floating up to the surface. With a splash he rose into the air, hovering majestically in front of the group, the purple waters and his damaged scales cascading to the ground.

"There we go," Alahn said, shaking the last of his old scales to the ground, while fresh new ones replaced them, *"much better."* Alahn dropped to the ground and embraced his son.

"Thank God we got to you in time." Earl said.

"Thank God you're alright." Alahn replied. *"They were using you as a bargaining chip."*

"What now?" Earl asked. "Lloyd said Ezekiel wants to end the human race… start over with the cosmics. Is that true?"

"That's what he plans to do." Alahn agreed. *"How I'm not entirely sure. What I do know is we need to stop him. This Lloyd you mentioned; he was the one I was talking to. Where is he now?"*

"He held them off so we could get you here." Zahna explained. "He could be in danger. We should go help him out now that we've got you all patched up."

"I can get there fastest." Alahn said. *"Keep Earl safe."*

Alahn saluted goodbye, then hovered in the air then flew up the stairs and down the hallway, chasing the only other cosmic human. And as he flew away Earl bent down to inspect the tiny scales that had fallen off his father. They were very small and separated from the purple skin of a cosmic had a white look to them. In fact, they appeared very much like a grain of sugar.

CHAP**10**TER

This was all going horribly. They had lost more than half the men they brought and only two commanders including himself remained. Quanton and the kids were missing, as well as Karina. Not only that, but Ezekiel and Genesis still headed forward to the entrance giving Cyrus and his squad's only chance in retreat. The men had run out of the compound bunker and just kept running as the laughing Ezekiel fired more and more blasts of whatever it was at them. Naturally this had resulted in what remained of the team getting scattered, and Cyrus found himself alone outside the train station with just two field troops. The lady they had arrested behind the counter had also managed to escape in the ensuing chaos Ezekiel and Genesis had caused. Ezekiel was now striding through the town heading towards the Coated Pond. This was it. The end game. Ezekiel was only a few moments away from bringing death to all creatures and making the earth into a cosmic haven. But the worst part was how helpless Cyrus felt. He had brought his elite fighters and weapons and hadn't even put a dent in Ezekiel or his pet. There were only two things that Cyrus knew of that could stand up to Ezekiel. That cosmic he had released in the compound, and Lloyd Salt.

"He's away from the station," Cyrus said into his com, to whoever was left to listen. "Everyone regroup inside, and we'll figure out what to do from there."

He and the two men beside him made their way inside the train station, Cyrus praying there would be a solution to this madness.

***   ***

The realization was startling. I had been to many deductive skills and critical thinking classes at my unusual school, so naturally being a bit of a detective was part of the job. As I tried to ignore the dead bodies strewn on the floor, I began piecing together the events I had lived through in order to try to make sense of what Ezekiel was going to do to be an apocalyptic threat. Obviously, it involved cosmics, but why exactly, and how exactly? During my thoughts I recalled the night before, and how Earl showed me that when the pond glowed it disintegrated that rock. This was another strange trait to the pond besides the water sugar. Also, after they had found Alahn he had said that Ezekiel had a stash of cosmic waters, the only thing that could heal him. Could the cosmic water Ezekiel possessed be one and the same substance as the Coated Pond? I also remembered when Karina and I were at the aquarium and saw the tiny thing in the fish tank. I had deducted that to be a baby cosmic. So, in turn that would mean cosmics are aquatic creatures, that are capable of living through entering cosmic waters, when activated. Activated you say? As you can tell the pond only disintegrates objects when in glow, such as I only had those powerful capabilities when I tapped into the purple aura. Therefore, that could mean that cosmics still lived on earth, in the Coated Pond, and that's how Ezekiel got his hands on one. And if cosmics could survive the cosmic waters, but not anything else, what better way to rid the earth of every living thing but cosmics, than to flood with cosmic waters? There were still some unanswered questions, but not bad for my first term. However tremendously terrible for the world. I was about to climb the ladder out of the compound when I heard footsteps behind me. Turning around warily, I let my guard down after I saw it was just Alahn.

"Alahn." I said. "Nice to see you're back on your feet."

"Indeed." Alahn replied. "But no time to rest. We must hurry. Ezekiel has already left the compound."

I nodded and began climbing the ladder.

"The Coated Pond." I began, as he was following behind me. "I think Ezekiel plans to somehow flood the world with it."

"Because the cosmic waters will leave only cosmics left." Said Alahn. "Of course."

We arrived at the top, to see Cyrus and a few other men from my organization holding an emergency meeting in the station.

170

"Lloyd!" Cyrus said, walking over to me. "There are some things you need to know."

"Oh, believe me," I said, probably a bit too disrespectfully to the leader of my school. "I know more than enough, no thanks to you. I don't know if you knew about my certain abilities, and that's why you sent me here, or what, but I'm done with you guys keeping me in the dark. What gain would you get from that?"

Cyrus seemed hesitant to answer.

"You needed to discover it for yourself." was Cyrus's excuse. "your connection to the cosmics, to the purple aura. To master it you needed to go through all you have been through and find out who you are yourself."

"Yeah, whatever." I said. "Either way we're failing horribly at our job. We need to stop Ezekiel."

"Lloyd." I heard in my head. *"We're wasting time."*

 "Right." I replied. "Cyrus evacuate the area in case we fail. If that happens this town will be the first to fall."

Alahn and I pushed past him and exited the station.

"He must be heading towards the pond." Alahn said. *"I can get us there faster. Let me lift you up."*

I don't particularly like being picked up, but the next thing I knew Alahn hoisted me up, wrapped his arms around my chest, and took off in the air. I looked down and saw purple aura bursting from Alahn's feet, gaining us height and boosting us forward. We were *flying.*

171

"I didn't know purple aura could do that." I said.

'It's kinda how purple aura works.' Alahn said. "It's only limited to the will of the user."

'Speaking of which." I replied, trying the telepathic communication for the first time. "We're going to have to use every bit of it. We're over Coated Pond.

I can see Ezekiel."

"You ready for this kid?" Alahn said descending.

I didn't reply. Because, really, I had no idea. We landed on the ground with a thud behind Ezekiel and Genesis.

"Don't tell me," Ezekiel said turning around. "Yup, Alahn's still alive, and you too, kid. Veronica must have failed. Though I shouldn't expect any less from the "worthy one"."

I didn't quite know what he was talking about. All I cared about was that he was talking and not destroying the human race.

"We know what you're doing." I said. "Flooding the world with cosmic waters. But why? Why can't cosmics and humans coexist?"

"Because the humans took everything away from me!" Ezekiel bellowed. "For a long time, I blamed the Cosmics for stripping me of my rightful being, but then I realized- it wasn't the Cosmics who truly did it to me. It was the humans, corrupting my mind to their purposes, using me for their war. It was their fault for my punishment!"

While the conversation was continuing on, I was desperately trying to think of a plan to stop Ezekiel. I glanced at Alahn and could tell he was doing the same. However, something didn't make sense here. Ezekiel talked as though he lived through the time humans and Cosmics lived together. But he looked no more than thirty, and if that was the case there was no way he had lived to see the cosmic age on earth.

"How selfish can you be!?" I contested. "Committing genocide for something that happened to you in the past?"

Ezekiel's face was one contorted in anger and sorrow.

"You fool!" he said. "Just like all the rest. I am the *selfless* one here! All humanity has to offer is sin and suffering. Look at all the pain they cause each other every day! They haven't changed for all the centuries I've lived. Why do you think the Cosmics left? They understood the hopelessness of the human race and knew they could never live among them. And so, it was their fault that the Cosmics were hunted and consumed by the Others as well! You all deserve nothing better than what I'm giving you!"

Two things caught my attention. Ezekiel had lived for centuries, and there was another race called the Others. More confusion added to the table.

"The Others." Alahn said to me. *"Ezekiel mentioned those to me as well. Said they were out to kill Cosmics."*

I nodded, though I was still looking at Ezekiel.

"But you don't know we can't change!" I said, my voice becoming more defensive. As I thought of the immensity of evil in Ezekiel's plan the angrier I got. "Everyone has a future, a tomorrow in which they can strive to be better than the last. I'm here to make sure that future becomes a reality. You don't have the right to take all those tomorrows away!!"

"How dare you speak to me of right!" Ezekiel roared. "They didn't have the right to take my own blood away from me! They didn't have the right to take away Oliver Cast!"

Oliver Cast. Cast was the oldest family name we could track. And Oliver Cast was one specific we knew about. He out casted himself from the family and wandered aimlessly until his death. But apparently not. Oliver Cast had changed his name to Ezekiel and somehow had lived for centuries. But this also meant that this man I was standing in front of, the evil man I had been fighting my entire term, was *my* ancestor.

"But now Ezekiel has risen." Ezekiel continued. "The worthy one they created all those years ago has failed and I am victorious."

He extended his arms, and I dove to the side in anticipation of an aura blast, but instead found myself being wrapped up in a glowing, snaking line flowing from Ezekiel's hand. It tightened around my waist, having a burning touch and crushing the air from my body. The same was happening to Alahn.

"Now Genesis," Ezekiel said. "Only a true cosmic can create a gateway to the cosmic pool at the edge of the universe. And that is what I created you for. Fulfill your purpose."

Genesis nodded and bent down to the edge of the pond. I struggled against the aura rope that held me, but the more I did the more intense grew the pain it caused. Reverberating from my waist to all of my body, it was too much to bear. I could not escape. Genesis placed his hands under the water and its entire body began to glow. It was a bright white hue, shining so brilliantly that soon its body was unrecognizable. The pond soon followed suit and the white waters began to swell.

"Yes!" Ezekiel shouted in victory, winds picking up and blowing against his flapping grey suit. "After all these years of planning, of preparation, at last my dream is a reality."

Genesis stood up watching the rising waters as they splashed against his feet. The grass around the pond was singed at its touch. Alahn was desperately trying to free himself from the aura ropes around him, but to no avail. As a result, Ezekiel tightened them further. I cried out in pain as he did so.

"Enjoy the show worthy one." Ezekiel taunted. "After all you will survive it. In fact, I even considered offering you a position on the new earth, if you're willing to pledge supreme allegiance to me." "N-never." I managed.

"Then when I have completed my task," Ezekiel said, the water gaining speed as it flowed. "I will kill you, after I have done the same with Alahn."

The cosmic waters now covered more than half the grassy area around the pond. The log cabin that was once a water-sugar shop was being devoured, and the water brushing my feet and legs burnt off my shoes and the ends of my pants. Ezekiel was right about my being able to survive the waters, that being linked to my connection to the cosmics. But that was not what I was worried about right now. There was no end to the destructive waters. It was the apocalypse and I had a front row seat.

"He was right about one thing." Alahn's strained thoughts said. *"You are the worthy one Lloyd. I can sense the aura emitting from you. It is much greater than his. For his power is fake and yours is true. If anyone can stop him it's you."*

The words of encouragement did little. Suddenly I heard a gunshot over the howling wind. The next thing I knew Ezekiel was clutching his left shoulder, the pain of the bullet breaking his concentration and his aura ropes. As their grip released me, I stumbled to keep balance. Swiveling my head to the left I saw Quanton standing at the edge of the growing pond, with a pistol.

"Get out of here." He shouted over the noise. "I've got some more bullets to hold him off."

Ezekiel was still recovering from the sudden shock and Genesis was too focused on continuing to monitor the expansion of the pond to realize anything was amiss. Alahn and I took the opportunity to race away from the action and join the creeping back Quanton as the waters rose faster and faster. Qaunton was firing more shots at Ezekiel, but he had created an aura shield around himself as he was somehow healing his wound.

"Zahna, Karina, and Earl are helping Cyrus and his crew evacuate the premises." Quanton explained once we were near. "I'll stay here as long as I can. But you need to get out of here now!"

"You've gotta make a run for it too." I said, backing up with him as the water came ever nearer. "You won't last a second."

"Look," Quanton said, pointing to Ezekiel. "He's already practically recovered.

Unless I aid your exit, he'll trap you again and then we'll all be screwed. You need time to figure out your abilities, and I know you will. You were always my brightest student, Lloyd. Now go!" I reluctantly nodded.

"Yes professor." I said, as we would in the classroom.

As I turned to run away with Alahn, I heard a yelp from Quanton. Ezekiel had thrown an aura rope on his arm and was yanking him towards the water.

"Leave me!" he shouted over to us, as he struggled to not fall in the deadly liquid. He fired shots at Ezekiel which kept his other hand busy with shields rather than us. "Get out of here!"

Alahn was going to listen to him and grabbed my shoulders in preparation to fly off. But I was not so quick to obey. I had let many people perish during my term. Letting another, especially someone closer to me was unacceptable. The next terrifying moment seemed to enact itself in slow motion. I attempted to run out of Alahn's grip to go aid Quanton as Ezekiel pulled the finishing blow. Quanton stumbled forward into the air. He dropped his gun which sizzled in the water.

Then he himself fell in, headfirst, and I watched helplessly as his body was incinerated. Nothing changed despite my shouts of protest, and soon I was back in the air with Alahn. We flew far away from the scene, out of Ezekiel's sight. I held back the tears that were vying to escape. Even though we would often contest in trying to out-wit each other, Quanton was my favorite teacher, and a man with a life that should have lasted longer.

"I couldn't save him." I solemnly said, as Alahn and I descended towards the town. "Just like all those other people. Alahn… we- we just lost."

"I know kid." Said Alahn's sad thoughts. *"I know."* We spotted out Earl and landed next to him.

"Lloyd!"' he said, "You're back."

I nodded but said nothing. There was silence for a minute, as I figured Alahn was telepathically explaining everything to Earl.

"The waters… you didn't stop him in time."

Once again I nodded. Earl looked from me to Alahn.

"Well what do we do?" He asked, his voice very concerned. "They can't be contained, only a true cosmic can start and stop it…"

He trailed off and we all just stood there a moment, acknowledging the scale of our defeat. Finally, Earl spoke up.

"We got the police in on the evac plan." He explained. "The town being so small, a full train and Cyrus's helicopters did the trick. Zahna got away safely went to see her aunt… it's just us, the soldier guys you work with, and Ezekiel." Hearing footsteps approaching, we saw Zahna dashing up to us. Cyrus and Karina were right behind her.

"The pond has reached the nearest sidewalk." Zahna said. "It's destroying everything in its path. We don't have much time."

"This is all my fault." I said. "I couldn't get the full potential of my powers like Ezekiel seemed to have. He kept referring to me as the worthy one... but all I've done is fail so far."

"Where's Quanton?" Cyrus asked. "I thought he went to find you." I looked down at the ground.

"He's... gone." I admitted.

Cyrus didn't seem too distressed by the news.

"That's another man down." He said. "I hardly have any fighting force left." He looked towards me and grabbed my shoulders.

"Lloyd," he began. "You're our last hope. You were granted with these amazing powers, far beyond the capabilities of Alahn's, or even Ezekiel's, for this purpose."

"But I couldn't even save Quanton!" I snapped. "And look, Alahn can fly, and sense aura's, a bunch of stuff that I can't do. How am I more powerful than him, let alone capable of stopping Ezekiel?" Cyrus sighed, and took his hands from my shoulders.

"I think it's time I showed you something." He said.

Reaching inside his coat, he slid a small ancient looking slab of stone from an inside pocket. On it were written words.

"We found this tablet on a dig after getting word of mysterious activity in a cave. It was pulsing a glowing purple, and still does from time to time." Cyrus continued, handing me the tablet. "As far as we can tell it's self-mending any damage it took over its existence."

"But what is it?" I asked beginning to read the words.

"An eternal scroll, that every cosmic keeps to log his life," said Cyrus. "and that is Oliver Cast's."

Oliver Cast. The man Ezekiel used to be before becoming Ezekiel and living for centuries, and one of my ancestors.

"Don't read the whole thing," Cyrus said. "We haven't the time. Skip to a couple pages before the end."

Before I could ask how to do that on a stone tablet, it seemed to recognize Cyrus's command, and a wave of purple went over the tablet and the words were replaced. I began to read the eternal scroll, everyone looking over my shoulder to read it as well.

This is the last entry I shall ever put in this accursed thing. For I have been casted out from my own rightful blood. My attempt of world domination of both Cosmics and humans has failed. The blind fools couldn't see I was making the world a better place. As judgement they stripped me of my Cosmic side and left only the human part of my mother. Then they laid a curse upon me that this world shall live to regret. I was made forever to be an outcast, and granted eternal life through that curse, as no one can forever be something without living that long. The elder warlock capable of such magic caught

himself though and added that my powers shall return to one along my family line, a worthy one, that should I ever rise again in my never-ending life, he should be capable of stopping me. Then the cowards ran away from earth, very well the only thing that was saving them from the all-powerful Others and stripped everyone's mind of them ever being there. But I shall rise again. And not as Oliver Cast, the man who failed. As *Ezekiel*, the man who will be victorious.

When I had finished a page, the tablet would change to the next one all on its own. Once I was done reading, I gave it back to Cyrus, a bit wide eyed.

"You see Lloyd," Cyrus said. "You were born for this, set up for this all those years ago. Prove you are the worthy one."

I was still digesting all that I had read. Ezekiel, my great ancestor, used to be a human cosmic like me before everything went down, and the Cosmics used to live among the humans. It also mentioned that species of Others again, that earth was somehow protecting the Cosmics from. But the most monumental thing for me was that I was indeed born for this. I had inherited these powers because I was capable of stopping Ezekiel. Everyone around me was looking at me expectantly. Earl, Cyrus, Karina, Alahn, Zahna... they were all depending on me. I couldn't fail them and let them perish. I was Lloyd Salt, the one who would stop Ezekiel for good, and save the world from his nihilistic plans. I took time to look every one of my associates in the eye.

"Thank you," I said. "All of you. I couldn't do this without you guys."

I glanced over my shoulder and saw the cosmic waters destroying their first buildings as they were coming up on us.

"But you need to go now." I continued, perhaps changing the mood. "Everyone but Alahn. We can survive this, but you can't. Get clear of this town, and if we succeed, we'll come meet up again. If we fail... see you in the afterlife."

None of them protested this. Cyrus said they could all ride with him in his helicopter now that they had less troops to carry. Earl shook my hand goodbye, and Zahna nodded me off. I will admit I was disappointed there was no dramatic goodbye between us like in the movies. Ah well, it's not like I was brave enough to say anything to Zahna anyway. Alahn hugged his son, and then we watched them run off with Cyrus and Karina, before turning back to the advancing death sentence.

'What's the plan, Lloyd?" Alahn asked, raising his head as the waters got higher.

"I am good at those." I replied, desperately trying to think of a moderately good one. "But we're in a tricky position. Only a true cosmic can open and close the gateway to the "cosmic pool at the edge of the universe" which doesn't include either of us. However...."

An enormously insane idea popped into my head.

"Alahn," I began. "You said the purple aura is only limited to what you can figure out how to do with it, correct?"

"I did say that."

182

"Well, Genesis basically created a portal to the cosmic pool, and since we can't do that, do you think it's possible we can create a portal elsewhere?"

'Seems plausible, but to where, and how would it help us." I telepathically explained my plan to Alahn.

"That's risky." He replied. "And I'm not sure possible, and yet- I've got nothing better."

"Let's go with it then." I said. "But first I need to get adept at creating portals." The water was now rising as well as surging forward. We had very little time.

"I've never done it before." Alahn said. 'So, you're just as good as me. Any suggestions on how?"

"Just like how I linked myself to you in the mind void." I explained. "Think exactly where you want to go, and bridge yourself to there."

I didn't know if that would or wouldn't work, but was the best shot I had. Gathering purple aura all around my body, I began to glow as I concentrated on exactly where I wanted to end up. Once I had the image completely in my brain, I created a circle with my glowing hands. It expanded into a hole big enough for me to walk into but didn't show any indication that it was a portal.

"Alahn," I said. "Help me out. I don't have enough power on my own."

"Where are you thinking of?' He asked, as I began to feel cold water splashing my feet.

"Right beside Ezekiel." I replied; my voice strained from keeping a consistent aura flow. "Now hurry!"

Alahn stood beside me and connected his power with mine. I imagined a bridge like I did in the mind void, connecting us to the spot where Ezekiel stood. With Alahn helping, the aura circle I had made swelled and vibrated, and emitted a great flash before showing where Ezekiel stood.

"Alahn!" I exclaimed, opening my eyes to look at the portal. "We did it!"

'Quick!' Came the reply. "*I can't keep this up much longer.*"

Before our energy ceased, we dove into the circle. We appeared right beside Ezekiel, and the water being deepest there, skimmed my pants down to shorts. We then did the much easier task of closing the portal.

"What in the," Ezekiel said, startled. "Where'd you two—"

Before he could finish, I blasted him with an aura wave, sending him stumbling back. Nearly being submerged in the water, he used the purple aura to hover in the air like Alahn had.

"I've had enough of you boy," Ezekiel viciously said. "And you Alahn. Should have killed *you* way back."

Alahn leapt in the air heading straight on for Ezekiel, but at the last second his limbs were wrapped up in Ezekiel's aura bands bringing him to a stop. I tried to get Ezekiel from behind, but he apparently had anticipated that, and spun around whipping a huge wave of aura that hit me square in the chest. My entire rib cage burning, I was flung a few feet away to catch myself on my hands and knees in the water. Ezekiel shouted something I couldn't hear over the roaring water, then created something like that of a purple blade around his hand, and stabbed Alahn in the chest with it.

"Alahn!" I shouted, dashing back towards Ezekiel.

Alahn's tough scales were saving him for now, but much longer and he would be killed. That was something I was not going to let happen. Not to Earl's father after they had just reunited. Creating aura blasts in both of my hands I shot the ground and boosted myself in the air, readying a punch that would knock Ezekiel's teeth clear to Kansas. If I connected that is. Ezekiel extended his free hand towards me, and five aura ropes snaked out from it, grabbing me in midair. They curved and arched around my body, tightening themselves around every place they could. Ezekiel had centuries of experience, and practice with the purple aura, and even without Genesis Alahn and I seemed no match for him.

"Let me go!" I screamed at Ezekiel. "I won't let you take him too!"

Ezekiel looked towards my way as his aura spear dove deeper and deeper into Alahn. He seemed to be grinning.

"Ahh, Lloyd Salt," he said. "That is your name isn't it? The preordained worthy one. What a joke. Tell me, how many people have died under your care?" I struggled against the ropes but to no avail.

"NO!" I shouted back, anger filling my mind. "I didn't let them die. You killed them!"

Ezekiel shook his head.

185

"They were your responsibility." He continued. "But you just couldn't do it. This is on you, Lloyd Salt."

"You're wrong…" I said, my voice fading.

"Lloyd," I heard Alahn's thoughts say to me. He sounded like he was in excruciating pain. *"Don't let your guilt and doubt cloud your mind. He knows where your weakness is. He's just hitting you where it hurts. Use your emotion Lloyd… it'll be your greatest weapon."*

His voice stopped and his body was contorted in pain. Alahn was right. I couldn't let my uncertainty about the past effect the future. The fault was Ezekiel's. And I would be the one to put end to him. Purple aura flared to life around me as I thought of all the people I had to avenge. Mr. Richards, Anderson, the two maids, professor Quanton… they all fueled my strength against Ezekiel. My eyes glowed bright purple, my body an exuberant hue as well. I could see purple aura in the air, all around me. I used it to destroy Ezekiel's chains that held me, and then to fire a mighty blast that knocked Ezekiel tumbling in the air, and Alahn out of his grasp. As Ezekiel righted himself, I concocted a vortex of aura around me, keeping me air born and providing me power.

"Why?" Ezekiel roared, an aura storm forming around him as well. "Why do you fight for such insignificant creatures?"

"Because you're right," I replied, intensifying the aura around me. "I'm not worthy. No one is. I fight because I believe the world can become a better place and won't if we don't try. Rather than destroying it, I'm trying to fix it. I fight to avenge all those you have hurt, and I fight for all those that you would hurt. That is why, Ezekiel, you will fall."

"YOUR NOTHING!" Ezekiel raged.

"No." I said, closing my eyes in preparation for the upcoming battle.

"I'm Lloyd Salt."

As I gathered all power available to me, I emitted an enormous bright flash, that Ezekiel even shielded his eyes. The wind was howling, the waves roaring, and streaks of purple aura striking the ground as though lightning.

"FACE ME EZEKIEL!" I shouted with everything I had.

We both flew towards each other, into a collision fiercer than anything had been before.

***   ***

Earl sat in a helicopter beside Zahna, flown by Cyrus. They had a great and horrifying view of the Coated Coast. The cosmic waters had gained height as well as length, and even the largest of buildings were swallowed up and destroyed. Much to his disappointment all Earl could do was watch from above, and hope his father and Lloyd found a way to stop it. After all the world hung in the balance. Just a couple weeks before Earl would have wanted nothing to do with such action, but now he wished he could be down there helping. After his father was declared missing, some boldness, some bravery had sprung up in him. After all he had come alone to a foreign town to look for him with only a backpack and a wad of money.

187

"I hope they're all right." Zahna said. "Alahn and Lloyd."

Earl turned his head to face her. Zahna was pretty, but he had always been more into taller girls, whereas Zahna was average at best. He could tell Lloyd liked her though.

"Yeah." He replied. "Ezekiel's insanely powerful. Though you seemed kind of ticked at Lloyd the last time you were together."

"Not really. A little bit. He just wouldn't explain who he was and took charge of us like he was some general or something. I don't know. Just got on my nerves a little."

"Personally, I like his take charge personality." Earl disagreed. "Gave me a bit of confidence you know?"

Zahna looked out the window.

"Perhaps I was a bit rude." She said. "Gosh look at the town. It's a wreck."

"I thought it was abandoned before," said Earl. "But after this I don't think anyone's coming back. I mean who's heard of a pond flooding on this type of scale?"

Zahna nodded.

"No kidding. I don't know where my aunt and I are going to go now."

"That does pose a problem." Earl said. "Perhaps—"

But he couldn't speak any more for the shock that suddenly came over him. A bright flash had sliced right through the helicopter, not harming it any, but it was so brilliantly bright Earl felt he might be blinded. In addition, it felt powerful, *electrified,* surging through his body and making all his hairs stand on end. Looking out the window he saw two glowing figures, hovering over the pond, heading full speed towards each other.

CHAP**11**TER

Alahn tumbled about the rapid waters, banging his head here, smashing his back there. Getting stabbed by an aura spear was incredibly painful and took some recovering from. He let his body go limp and let the water carry him while he healed himself in the cosmic waters. Lloyd had finally seemed to realize the extent of his powers and was using them to their full potential. Earth still had hope after all. However what Lloyd planned to do to save it, Alahn was unsure about. Suddenly a surge of energy ran through him. He began sensing aura readings beyond anything he had sensed before. Whatever was going on up there, it was big. Alahn got the feeling that whatever it was, it would decide the fate of the world.

***   ***

It was a thunderous, enormous boom that resulted from Ezekiel's and my crash. Our aura storms combined into each other, creating one double the size of a singular. Inside we duked it out, using the aura around us to keep us air born. For the most part Ezekiel had the upper hand, for being older and stronger than me his punches hurt me more than mine hurt him. I did have one advantage though. He did not expect me to have honed my powers as much as I had, and I was able to catch him off guard with clever tricks I had learned. Ezekiel hurled a giant aura ball my way, which I was able to catch in my hands and throw back. Ezekiel flew out of the way and dove towards me. Returning the dive, we tumbled into each other and somersaulted around the vortex. Ezekiel viciously threw his fists at me, while I desperately tried to dodge and throw my own. My knuckles connected with his chin, which seemed to slow him down very little, for he instantly grabbed for my neck to put me in a choke hold. I created an aura shield around me, and he recoiled at the burning touch. Taking advantage of this, I followed up by making a spear around my hand as I had seen Ezekiel do to Alahn and stabbed him in the chest. Ezekiel shouted in pain, before his hands glowed purple, and he painstakingly pulled the spear from his body. He then raised his hand in the air, and out of the swirling vortex came multiple purple lightning bolts heading my way. I did not have time to either avoid, or defend against all of them, and one of them hit me square in the back. It sent me flying and I had to consciously stop myself from being flung out of the vortex completely. Pain was erupting all around my shoulders and upper back, so I had to take a moment to gather myself. Ezekiel however was still going strong, and my resting was cut short by having to leap out of the way of another aura blast. Ezekiel seemed tireless, but I for one was exhausted. It was clear by now I could not beat him by brute force. I would have to formulate one of my famous plans that had saved me before. However, that was quite hard as I was constantly trying not to die. After Ezekiel had struck me with the lightning though, I got an idea. It was quite simple, but the hard part would be surviving long enough to execute it. Allowing myself to be hit by an aura blast from Ezekiel, I was pushed to the edge of the vortex. Staying there, I now participated in a long-range battle where I just dodged for most of it. Ezekiel soon got frustrated, and as I had hoped created some of his aura ropes to hold me. Once again, I let myself become subject to his attack, and now rendered immovable, he advanced towards me.

"You're slowing down, Lloyd." Ezekiel said, his hands glowing. "You put up an entertaining fight though. I'll enjoy choking the life from your body."

He surged forward to grab my neck in a fatal grasp that I could not escape. If he had connected, I would have been killed and the world would have perished. Fortunately, I for once knew something Ezekiel didn't. When he had wrapped the aura ropes around me, I had secretly created a tiny aura shield around my arms. The ropes weren't actually around my body so I could easily tear them apart with the power of my shields. This I did when Ezekiel was a moment away from wringing my neck, and I grasped hold of his shoulders and threw him headfirst out of the vortex. I followed suit, but purposely exited the storm, so I was prepared to start the flying technique that Alahn had learned. Dispensing purple aura from my feet I continued to keep myself aloft. Ezekiel however was not ready for the sudden change of atmosphere and was falling through thin air. Diving down towards him, I didn't want to give Ezekiel a chance to think. Forming a giant aura blast, I caught up to him and slammed it down on his chest. Ezekiel plummeted to the ground below, smashing smack dab in the middle of a cement road. Nothing could survive a fall like that. I had beaten Ezekiel like I had beaten all the other villains in this town. I had outsmarted him. Having no time to bask in the glory though, I flew down to the center and source of the cosmic waters and began searching for Alahn. The aura vortex above began to dissipate with nothing charging it. Once I was near ground level, I began calling for Alahn.

"Alahn!" I broadcasted as far as I could. *"Alahn are you alright? I defeated him!*

We need to do the plan before it's too late!" I waited a few seconds before calling again. *"Alahn! Are you—"*

"Right here." I heard.

Alahn rose from the waters in front of me.

"Sorry I couldn't help." He said. *"I had to heal after the encounter with Ezekiel. Did you beat him?"*

"Yes." I said out loud, now that he was in ear shot. I prefer the normal way of talking. "Now we need to do the plan quick!"

"*Incredible.*" Said Alahn. "*Are you sure it'll work? It could be dangerous.*"

"*That* is dangerous." I said, pointing to the source of the waters. They were so high now you couldn't even see Genesis keeping them going. "It's the best shot we've got. But I don't think I'm powerful enough to do it alone. I'll need your help."

Alahn nodded.

"*I'm with you, Lloyd.*" He said.

"Good." I replied. "You know what to do. On my word."

We flew up to right above where the water was dispensing. Alahn was right. My plan was a bit dangerous. I got the idea from the portal creating Genesis had done to the cosmic pool. Just like we had done to get to Ezekiel, Alahn and I were going to combine our power to create another portal. But this time over a much larger distance. My plan was to create a small portal to the center of a black hole, so that it would suck up the cosmic waters, and get them off the earth. While it was doing this, we would go and stop Genesis so that he could no longer create a portal to the cosmic pool, and put an end to this madness.

"Ready?" I asked Alahn. It was a rhetorical question, and I didn't wait for the answer. "Now!"

We both bridged our position to a black hole in our minds and used our aura powers to create a portal there. The distance was so great though, it took more time and energy than the last portal we had created, and I wasn't sure if we could pull it off. I gritted my teeth as I offered more and more power to the creation of the portal. A small circle appeared, and inside it was utter darkness. Strong winds began to pick up, and I felt the portal sucking me in towards it. We had successfully created a portal to the center of a black hole. "RUN!" I shouted, as the black hole's pull got stronger.

Alahn and I tried to fly away from the black hole, but it was not easy. For a horrifying moment I thought we would be sucked in and torn apart, but we were able to just make it out of range of the pull and fly away. I turned back to see the black hole sucking up the dispensing cosmic waters. No more was being added to the earth. We had done it!

"Alahn!" I said, laughing in joy. "We did it!"

"Indeed, we did." Alahn replied. *"You were the worthy one, Lloyd."*

"We're not done yet though." I said, beckoning towards the ground. The waters which had been thick before, were thinning out thanks to the black hole. You could now see Genesis looking up very irritated at the black hole. "We still have Genesis to deal with."

We flew down and landed on the ground. I winced as some sharp rocks dug into my bare feet, the cosmic waters having burned off my shoes before. We approached Genesis, who thankfully was just out of range of the black hole's pull.

"Genesis!" I announced. "Your 'father' is gone. Your mission has been thwarted. There's nothing else for you to do but come with us peacefully."

Genesis looked us up and down, with our arms outstretched and ready to fire aura blasts.

"If father truly is gone," it put into Alahn's and my head. *"Then I am my own creature."*

With that it promptly flew off into the sky. Before Alahn and I had time to react, it was far out of sight.

"It retreated?" I said.

The portal to the cosmic pool closed with nothing tending it, and the black hole continued to suck in the overflowing waters. With no more water coming out, the earth had nothing more to worry about. We had saved the world.

"Perhaps it didn't have any choice but to obey Ezekiel." Alahn suggested. *"After all it was programmed by him. Perhaps now that it's no longer a slave, it wants to do what it pleases rather than what Ezekiel does."*

"I guess so." I agreed. "Should we try to go after it?"

"No." Alahn said. *"There's only one place it could be going. I sensed another hold out of Cosmics in the Atlantic. That's the only place on earth it'll fit in. I think without the evil grip of Ezekiel it'll live a peaceful life among its kind."*

"If you say so." I replied. "This... other hold out of Cosmics. What are they doing?"

"They're not fully developed." Alahn said. *"I've tried to communicate with them. They're still infants. Cosmics grow at a different pace than*

humans. They remain infants until entering a cocoon. When they emerge they are full grown.

Ezekiel sped up this process in the lab using electric treatment. For now, they remain infants."

"All this is so weird." I said. "I'm related to aliens that live on earth, with strange abilities and lives. At least Ezekiel's gone."

"Gone?" A ragged voice said from behind. I turned to see a battered, bleeding,

Ezekiel barely standing. "Lloyd, I still plague you."

"Ezekiel!" I exclaimed in shock. "But, how—"

"Before you did your little black hole trick," Said Ezekiel. "The cosmic waters reached me. I was able to heal before I perished completely."

"Give it up." I said, raising my glowing hands. Alahn did the same. "You're outnumbered and beat."

"Outnumbered, maybe." He said. "Out powered? I don't think so."

He flung an aura rope at Alahn that struck him exactly where Ezekiel had stabbed him before. The rope slid inside Alahn easily, and once it was there, he didn't move an inch.

"You see," Ezekiel continued. "I weakened the scales on Alahn's chest so much that they're near useless. I move this rope a fraction it penetrates his heart.

So, I suggest Lloyd, you don't move a fraction either."

I stayed put.

"Ezekiel it's over." I bargained. "Your plan failed. You have nothing to gain from this."

"Except hurting you." He said, grinning vilely. He looked up at Cyrus's helicopter circling above. "Up there is your girl, your friend, and your leader." With his free hand he charged a powerful aura blast. "I could blast them from here, and they all perish. You see Lloyd, you take away my world I take away yours."

He released the blast.

"NO!" I said, charging my feet and flying into him.

Later I realized this very well could have killed Alahn, but thanks to one thing science never can and never will explain, coincidence, the aura rope came out just right to keep him from dying. When I crashed into Ezekiel his aim was just messed up a little bit, but I prayed it would be enough to keep it from hitting the copter. I grabbed hold of Ezekiel's waist, and brought him into the air with me. In my blind attack, I didn't see that we were heading straight for the black hole. I felt the pull of it bringing us in. Getting much closer to it than last time, I felt the cold water getting sucked in against my back. I went to fly away, dropping Ezekiel, but this time he grabbed hold of me.

"You're coming with me, boy." He growled.

I used all the power I had to fly away, but with the combined might of Ezekiel's hold, and the black holes pull, it was to no avail. Ezekiel was laughing that evil laugh of a villain as I struggled to get away. I got an idea, an idea much more gruesome than I preferred, but when you're about to die you'll do just about anything. Creating an aura blade around my right hand, I brought it down in a crushing blow and cut off both of Ezekiel's hands. He howled in rage as he was sucked further into the black hole. His back ran along the cosmic waters going into the hole as well before he himself disappeared into the hole of darkness.

"May the Others consume you." Was the last thing Ezekiel said. *"May they consume you all."*

And then Ezekiel was gone. I would have flown away, but another task had befallen my mind. The black hole had to be closed or else it would continue sucking things into no end. I let myself to be pulled in closer than I liked to the black hole, and right before I was sucked in completely, I closed it the same way I closed the other portal. Blasting a consistent aura flow at it, then clasping my hands together. It successfully closed, and I began falling back down through the air. The water it had been sucking up fell with me, settling back into the divot in the ground to create a normal pond again. The energy I used up to create and close the black hole, not to mention battle Ezekiel, had really taken it out of me. I was much too exhausted to fly again, and my body fell limp into the Coated Pond below me. I sunk down in the waters as I slipped unconscious.

***   ***

I awoke to a warming and calming green glow. I opened my eyes, quite surprised I hadn't drowned in the water. I found myself inside an air bubble being created by... Genesis? At least it looked exactly like it. But how? I had seen Genesis fly away. The cosmic was sustaining the air bubble so I could breathe, and was clutching a green, pulsating orb in its hands. Genesis (or whatever it was) slowly pushed the green orb into my head. I felt a surge of power flowing through my veins, before blacking out again.

***   ***

I found myself dazed and lying on the edge of ground beside the Coated Pond. I felt like something had happened, but I couldn't remember what. The last thing I recalled was closing the black hole and falling… how did I get here? Not worrying too much about it, just grateful that I was alive, and the world was still standing, I stood and shakily ran over to Alahn's body that was lying on the ground.

"Alahn?" I said. "You still with us?"

"Yes." Came the reply as I was flooded with relief. *"Just give me a minute."*

Alahn scooped up a bit of water residue that was still on the ground and put it to his chest. The water glowing a blue hue, it healed the wound. Alahn stood shakily to his feet.

"I did it Alahn." I said. "It's over."

With nothing happening, and no life around it was eerily silent. The Coated Pond ceased glowing as it reverted to normal water. Alahn and I just stood there a moment in silence, enjoying the calm. Soon the sound of a helicopter could be heard, and Cyrus's copter landed on the grass behind us. Earl and Zahna jumped out, followed by Cyrus and Karina.

"Lloyd!" Earl said, running up. "You did it!" Zahna was right behind him.

"That was pretty freaky." She said. "Yeah." I agreed. "My heart's still racing." Cyrus placed his hand on my shoulder.

"This mission cost some good men." He said. "But I knew I could count on you."

I didn't respond to Cyrus. I was still upset with his logic of not telling me anything.

"Now this town is *really* derelict." She said winking.

I smiled. Now that I knew her ditzyness was just an act before, she was much more tolerable.

"What are we going to do with Veronica?" I asked, the question suddenly coming to me.

"After you came up from the compound, I figured you had somehow neutralized her." Cyrus replied. "Sent some men down to see if there was any way to bring her in. They found her dead with a hole through her chest in a containment cell. She must have committed suicide." I nodded grimly.

"These guys seem to be under the "dead better than captured" philosophy." Cyrus continued. "The police said Michael Stane was killed after they brought him in."

"Those connected to the purple aura can sense others that are as well," Alahn said. *"After Ezekiel was trapped in the black hole Veronica probably could no longer sense his connection and figured he failed. She must have thought there was nothing left to live for."*

I just shook my head. This whole caper had resulted in too much death. I tried to think of something to say to lighten the mood.

"You know what's odd though?" I said. "After all the events with the Coated Pond, I still don't know what the water-sugar was all about."

Earl stepped forward.

"I might know the answer to this one." He said. "After we healed my dad in Ezekiel's small cosmic water collection, he shed a bunch of small white scales.

To the untrained eye they might look like grains of sugar." I looked at him in amazement.

"So, your saying," I began. "That the infant Cosmics that used to live in this pond were shedding scales that washed up like salt, that tasted like... sugar?" Earl nodded.

"So, all this time people have been seasoning their food with, and tasting scales?"

We all had a laugh at this.

"The cosmic infusion in them probably made them taste good." Alahn said.

"How hilarious."

"Well," Cyrus said. "I don't think anyone's coming back to this town, and it's time we leave too. Zahna we'll drop you off with your aunt, with whom you will not share a word about this or anyone else for that matter, understood?

We have punishments we can set in order if you do." Zahna nodded. Cyrus then turned to Earl.

"Earl we can bring you back to your mother, but your father being how he is now, may have to stay with us." Earl looked mortified.

"But—" He began.

"*Son.*" I heard Alahn tell him through his thoughts. "*I cannot return to a normal human life, for I am now part Cosmic. However, mister Cyrus,*" Alahn looked at Cyrus. "*I'm not coming with you either. I cannot live without a daily dose of cosmic water. I am going to the other deposit of Cosmics in the Atlantic, to live among them once they are grown. Perhaps I shall even find Genesis there.*"

"But dad!" Earl protested. "I just found you! Now you're going to go off to some unknown, like, house of Cosmics?"

Alahn put his hands-on Earl's shoulders.

"*I will visit you often.*" He said to him. "*But please do not mention this to your mother. She has already come to terms with my disappearance. I love you son. Take care of your mother.*"

Then he flew off the same direction as Genesis. Earl had tears in his eyes, but he held it together.

"Very well then." Cyrus said. "Shall we get going?"

203

We were soon loading up in the big helicopter. Before I hopped in I took one last look at the pond. So much had happened to me in this town. I went to make my hands glow, almost like a sign off to the town. But nothing happened. I tried to make my shield. Once again nothing.

"Lloyd," Cyrus said, poking his head from the driver's seat. "You coming?"

"My powers," I said. "They're gone." Cyrus looked at me up and down.

"Curious." He said. "They gave the bloodline back to the family to combat Ezekiel, so now that its purpose is done, perhaps the cosmic blood has been taken away again."

I just shrugged. Oddly I found no great loss in this. I'm not sure how I would have lived life knowing I had that kind of power anyway. I boarded the helicopter, and I watched as the town faded out of sight. The cosmic waters had really destroyed it. All that was left were smoldering buildings. So long Coated Coast. Our first landing was at the Chicago train station where we dropped off Zahna to go find her aunt and figure out where to live.

"Remember," Cyrus told her. "You can't breathe a word of any of this to anyone. We have ways to find out and ways to punish." Zahna just nodded.

"See ya, Lloyd." She said as she left. "Just so you know, you definitely rank high on the coolest boys I've met."

I took that sentence to heart. I felt a strange sense of disappointment as we left Zahna. Even though I didn't know her that well, if I ever *liked* a girl it would have been her. Before she left Cyrus had oddly, and kind of out of place, patted her shoulder. I knew that he was placing a tracker and radio com to listen in on her conversations, making sure she said nothing of the agency or of the true events that occurred at the Coated Coast. If she did slip to someone, proper punishments would be put in order immediately. As we went to the town where Earl said he lived in, he mentioned how he still had a couple days before his mom expected him home from his out of state grandma.

"I was lucky my grandma didn't have a phone or internet so she couldn't expose me," Earl said. "But I may have to blow my cover myself."

"Just convince her you actually said the amount of days you were gone." I said.

"That's always worked for me."

"Where do you sneak off too?" Earl asked doubtfully.

"I've never tried the excuse." I said. "So therefore, it's never failed. So – it's never not worked for me."

Earl laughed and punched me lightly in the shoulder.

"I still might try it though." He said.

We dropped him off in his home city of Springfield, a few blocks away from his house. As he gathered his bags and was ready to depart, he gave me a fist bump.

"The same goes for you Mr. Alten." Cyrus began, fixing Earl with the same stare he gave Zahna. "Not a word."

"Yes sir." Earl replied. Cyrus did a less awkward shoulder pat on him as well, positioning another microscopic listening and tracking chip.

"It's been a pleasure working with you." I said to Earl.

"Any time," Earl replied. "But preferably not for a while."

We waved goodbye, before heading back to my school, where all this began as a simple term, a test to see if I was worthy to graduate. It was a silent ride, as I spent it all being afraid for all those times, I had to ignore my fear in Coated Coast. The main school building I attended came into view, hidden as a rich man's mansion in the forest. It had no signs or labels, as this branch of the C.I.A. was of the most secretive. Only few knew of the Intellectual and Military Schooling Organization. There I met my mom and dad who embraced me.

"We knew this term was more dangerous than average." My mother said. "But they were certain you could handle it with Karina."

I could tell Cyrus hadn't told her the whole bit. He did announce though, that I had not only passed, but gained the highest score possible on my term. This earned me many congratulations from my parents. We returned home, where my mother cooked up a celebratory dinner. I shared stories with them about what I had done on my term, many times masking the truth. For that was how the organization rolled. Always masked in secrets, even to its own allies. Yes, indeed the family business was complicated. I still knew very little about it, or what my future would come from it. In that day I knew one certainty; I am a kid from Chicago who wants to make the world a better place, with a brighter future for all.

I am Lloyd Salt.

EPILOGUE

The following night...

Cyrus descended a staircase, heading towards his private chamber. He arrived at the bottom to be faced with a mechanically opening door, and a fingerprint scanner. Pressing his right hand against the screen, he waited while it confirmed who he was. For no one else but he was granted entrance down here. The door emitted a beep and swung open. Cyrus, checking that no one was following behind him, entered, and the door shut behind him. The room he was now in was empty save for a small table in the center.

Checking his watch, he waited until the last minute was up until they would meet; the watch placed its hand on midnight. Suddenly above the table, a blue swirling circle appeared, the face of a cosmic looking through it.

"All went as you said it should." Cyrus said. "Lloyd did not find out about his abilities until his third day in the Coated Coast. Quanton perished, and Alahn went to live in the fallen city of Atlantis with you."

The cosmic looked as though it was grinning, if it had a mouth.

"Yes. The future has changed around me as it should." It said. *"I went back to your time and made sure the boy obtained the Entity of Knowledge. All is as should be, but I will continue to need your help to keep it this way."* Cyrus nodded.

"Whatever you need." He said. "You've told me what the future could be, and I approve. I assume everything still revolves around Lloyd Salt?"

"Yes. In four years' time another important event will need our assistance." The cosmic replied. *"He is the key to both destroying or blessing the future. I have seen both possibilities through the Entity of Time. Together, Cyrus, you and I shall strive for the best outcome. For I only wish to see a perfect future."*

"It will be done," Cyrus said, as the swirling circle closed, and the cosmic faded from view. "You'll continue to work through me, Genesis."

The Life of Lloyd Salt Continues

Made in the USA
Columbia, SC
15 October 2020